PRAISE FOR *JONAH MAN*

"Chris Narozny has ̲ ̲ ̲ ̲ ̲ ̲ ̲ ̲ ̲ ̲ ̲ ̲ ̲
20th-century ink and come up with a wo.. I
couldn't oversell. Full of backflips, hook hands, bad drugs, busted
acts and rag-tag beauties burning out before uncaring audiences
under the glare of calcium lights, *Jonah Man* sings its story from
deep in the throat, tells it from the gut, casts it into hard-won,
hytone prose, tosses it growling and sparking onto the sticky
asphalt, lets it bandy twist and barrel turn in the sizzling rain,
the jaw-dropped sun."—**Laird Hunt**, author of *Ray of the Star*
and *The Impossibly*

"If William Faulkner and Cormac McCarthy got together to
write a novel about vaudeville, it would probably be something
like Chris Narozny's *Jonah Man*."—**Michael Kimball**, author of
Dear Everybody and *Us*

"What can we learn from exceptionally talented orphans, one-
handed, moonlighting jugglers, and inspectors who proceed by
the light of accidents? A great deal indeed. In the enigmatic
language of vaudeville, *Jonah Man* posits readers at the
crossroads with an invitation to consider the gaps between who
we have been and who we might, still, become. A remarkable
achievement, this book is a dream. And like all powerful dreams,
it has the power to wake you."—**Selah Saterstrom**, author of
The Meat and Spirit Plan and *The Pink Institution*

Jonah Man

Jonah Man

CHRISTOPHER NAROZNY

PUBLISHING

BROOKLYN, NEW YORK

APR 1 2 2012

Fic
Nar

Printed in the United States of America
10 9 8 7 6 5 4 3 2 1

Ig Publishing
392 Clinton Avenue
Brooklyn, NY 11238
www.igpub.com

Library of Congress Cataloging-in-Publication Data

Narozny, Christopher.
Jonah man / Christopher Narozny.
    p. cm.
ISBN 978-1-935439-48-6
1. Vaudeville--United States--Fiction. I. Title.
PS3614.A698J66 2012
813'.6--dc23
                                        2011051469

For Nina

I

SWAIN

Chicago, Illinois

September 5, 1922

I'm in the wings, watching Jonson and his boy. Mostly I'm watching the boy. Father and son are done up in rags, dancing atop wooden barrels. It's something everyone's seen before and no one minds seeing again. But then a calcium light spots the boy. He shuffles faster, windmilling his arms, gathering speed before he thrusts his feet out from under him. He spins through a backflip, lands flatfooted on his barrel, still singing, still wind-milling.

The audience applauds, but the boy's barely started. He lifts himself into a handstand, taps his feet on the air above him, singing out from between his arms, upside down, sounding as good as he did right side up. People rise, whistle. Nobody can look away. The boy is a hytone note on a bill of hokum. Jonson is in the shadows now, clapping—sober, because this is a morning show.

The curtain falls and I walk along the edge of the stage, take my place on the olio. The audience is still standing for the boy. I wave my hook at them, open my valise, start both the striped and unstriped balls turning in the air. I use the curved side of my hook like the palm of a hand, get two, then three, then four balls circling in front of me. An old man in the front row stands to leave. More follow.

The pianist starts vamping in the pit. I balance a ball on the flat of my hook, keep the others going with my good hand. One by one I bring the balls to rest, one atop the other on top of my hook. I bow my head, the column holding steady at the end of my hacked arm.

Jonson greets me offstage with a Dutch-uncle sneer that says I'm a fool to keep trying. In the weeks since he joined the bill, it's always his face watching from the wings.

Top-notch chasing, he says. Even cleared the gallery.

I set down my valise, stand so the toes of our shoes are touching. Jonson folds his arms over his dished chest.

Where would you be without your boy? I ask.

Retired, he says. He holds his laughter for a beat, then erupts in burlesque peals.

• • •

It's what's right, I say.

It's what can't happen, the manager says. The order's the order. I bump you up, someone else is unhappy.

Since when does a fresh act get top billing?

You've seen the kid?

Yes.

All right, then.

But I've done my time. I have a good act, but it's not a finale.

Doesn't have to be. An audience needs something to wind them back down.

• • •

Backstage, property men pace the set with pots of glue and gilt paint, touching up the plywood throne, the receding archways and corridors stenciled on the drop. One of them peers through a part in the curtain. I walk into the wings, see Jonson's boy rehearsing on the olio. Jonson sits stage left in the front row, smoking a Hermosa and drinking from a tin flask. The boy stub-toe walks along the edge of the stage, then launches into a series of heel scuffs and buck breaks, turning the lip of the boards into a ledge, lurching as though he might topple forward. Each time it seems he's gone too far, he reels himself back, pantomimes relief. It's a balance act, designed to take control of the audience's breathing, to make them gasp and laugh in quick succession. I glance at Jonson. He's watching me watch his son. He smiles, nods toward the stage, raises his flask. I shift my eyes back to the boy. He's near the center of the olio now, standing with one leg locked, ad-libbing with his active foot. There's technique and sweat, but nothing an audience would take for effort. The manager is right. Runt letters won't hold the boy's name much longer.

I pick up my valise, head to my dressing room. The contortionist is seated on a wood stool, stripped to his underclothes, rubbing down his legs with a rank-smelling poultice. Twenty years of double splits and slides have left his spine scuted like a reptile's. We're bookends on the bill, opening and shut, something for people to look at while they walk the aisles. In the days of nickel theaters, Roy took the stage at six feet tall and ended his act coiled inside a shallow water bucket. Now he works with a trunk the size of a child's coffin.

Kill 'em? he asks.

They ran off, I say.

He grimaces, leans back on his stool, waits for a spasm to pass. Our patter is just noise where the questions should be. How many jumps before we're struck from the rolls? Is it all just luck and pull, or is there something we should have understood years ago? I flip through the back pages of a dated *Variety* while he wrangles into an aqua body suit. It isn't long before the house boy rings his bell and Roy stands.

Merde, I say.

He nods. As he shuts the door behind him, I see he's left the middle buttons of his suit undone.

I have time until it's my turn again. I angle Roy's stool under the door knob, open my day bag, lift out a spare hook and balance it on my knee. From the socket, I pull down an eye-dropper, a glass vial, a doctor's needle. I thumb the top from the dropper, work the needle through the nipple. I transfer two beads of silver-blue liquid from vial to dropper, then put the cap back on with the syringe in place. I insert the needle beneath a nub of bone in my stump. Eyes shut, I feel a warmth spread through my body, another person's skin enveloping my own.

Roy returns, sweating through his suit.

How's the house? I ask.

Handcuffed.

He looks me over.

You might want to lay off, he says.

Off what?

All right, he says. Not my affair.

I wait in the wings with my back to the stage while the audience applauds the boy.

On the olio, I stare into the spot, unblinking.

. . .

My hotel room is just a bed and window with floors and walls that don't stop the smallest sound. I shut the curtain, jostle my stub from the hook, peel off the stump sock. The flesh beneath retains an impression of the gauze. I blow the sweat dry, chafe away flecks of dead skin.

I swallow a soporific, then fall backwards onto the bed. I can't push the boy's act from my mind. Anyone who's spent time on the boards can see him inventing, testing, searching for something his body won't do. The audience is just so many faces sloping upward. Subtract them and he'd still perform.

My pulse starts to stutter, my muscles spasm. I get up, drag the copper bed frame so it's blocking the door, unlock my largest valise. There are trails of boric acid leading from where the bedposts used to be. The valise is packed with prosthetics—seven in all—different colors, different shaped hooks. I pick one up, slide out a glass vial. The blue is still dark, still swirling around the silver. I pull a rag from a second socket, turn it over until I find a spot that isn't stained. I flick off the stopper, touch the vial to the rag. With my finger on the back side of the fresh stain, I rub the rag over my gums, the roof of my mouth, the underside of my tongue. I stand the vial on the floor, take up my canteen, spill a drop of vinegar into the silver-blue liquid and replace the stopper.

I lie on the bed and wait, my lips burning. Soon, there's a burgeoning in my right wrist—a sprouting. I feel flesh and bone brushing aside soil, joints flexing and stretching their way through dirt.

. . .

In the morning, I head out with a package of six vials, one in each pants pocket, one in each sock. I'm wearing my street prosthetic—a hook with little curve, straight enough to cut like a knife. I take the money I was told to spend on a taxi, buy a half-pot of coffee, four eggs over easy, a small stack of pancakes. The girl behind the counter eyes my hook. I use it to slice through the buttered and syruped batter, then lick the metal clean. She stops staring.

I find the street number written in white along the side of a forest-green porte-cochere. The concierge looks up from whatever he's reading. There's a cicatrized gash circling his neck above the collar. I stroke the palm-sized fronds of a potted tree while he places the call.

The buyer is waiting in the hall, smoking a cigarillo and wearing a bathrobe with no sash. He takes a wallet from his pocket, thumbs through the bill fold. His hands look as if they've been pumped full of water and rubbed raw. His chest is spotted with white stubble. I glance up the hall. There's a peephole drilled above each knocker.

Inside, I say.

He leads me into a narrow vestibule, then turns and holds up his hand. Behind him a living space sprawls out in all directions. I hear a woman who's maybe humming—or it may be two women, one of them or someone else playing ragtime on a piano. A painting of an oblong figure with skin the color of Ray's body suit hangs on the far wall.

Nice place, I say.

The vials, he says, pushing the bills at me. Bits of ash flake down onto his chest.

I count his money, dig the vials from my pockets and socks. I make him tell me to leave.

Halfway back, I spot Jonson's boy staring in a shop window. There's no sign of Jonson. I hide my hook in my coat pocket, lower the brim of my hat, move closer. The boy's watching a brindled cat weave its way around the potted plants in a flower shop display case. He's all bone beneath the coat—his hair unwashed, slept on, his shoelaces untied. He looks like a true-life version of the hobo he plays on stage. It occurs to me that I might just tap him on the shoulder, say hello. But what I want to know he can't tell me. Not yet. Maybe when he's my age, looking back.

He starts walking. I keep a few strides behind. He won't

recognize me, not with my hook out of sight and my scalp covered. He stops again, this time at a bookseller's. There's an old hardback book spread open on a pedestal in the window, the pages scrawled over with foreign writing. The kid studies the text like he can read whatever language it might be written in, then steps inside. I watch him through the glass storefront. No one seems to notice him, not the bookseller standing behind the counter, not the few customers he slides by in one of the store's narrow aisles. He keeps his coat buttoned, walks slow, reading down the spines.

In the aisle closest to the door, he lifts a fat tome from its shelf, sits on a footstool, opens to a random chapter and begins reading. He reads until he's the store's only customer, then carries the book up front. Before the clerk can quote a price, the boy lifts a small paper bag from his coat pocket and sets it on the counter. The clerk weighs the bag in his palm, nods, opens his register and passes the boy an envelope. The boy exits the store, leaving his book behind.

We work our way towards the hotel, the brownstones turning to cinderblocks, the trees dropping off street-by-street until they're all but gone. He leads me to a dime museum. It's a converted storefront, the windows covered with posters of bearded women and tattooed strongmen. A sidewalk placard reads, *Oddities of All Nations*. The boy reaches into his pocket, pulls out a fistful of coins, plucks one off his palm. I tell myself to keep walking, but for a while I just stand there, thinking, seeing myself from someplace distant—a grown man following a boy through a city I barely know. But then the distance closes, and I step to the booth with my dime in hand.

Fifteen cents, the man says.

A joke?

Just trying to pass the day.

We wait in a cordoned-off area while the earlier house clears. There's a small gathering—college kids and day laborers on break—the kind of crowd that sits in the galleries and stomps their feet, shouting louder than the actors. I stand so the boy's back is to me. He raises up on his toes, straining to see over the partition. The soles of his shoes are worn to nothing. I keep my good hand in my pocket, fingers wrapped around the bills.

A man in a plug-opera hat unhooks the cord, waves us in.

Ladies and gentlemen, he says, I apologize for the delay. But I assure you that once inside, you won't want to leave.

We follow him into the curio hall—a narrow room with exhibits lined against one wall, separated by opaque scrims. The professor holds up his hand, stops us at the first cubicle. There's a glass jar filled with clear liquid sitting on a pedestal. There's an object suspended near the center of the jar. The wall behind is plastered with newsprint.

What have we here? he asks.

You tell us, says a kid in a lettered sweater.

Fair enough.

He taps the jar with his pointer, thumbs his spectacles up the bridge of his nose.

Here, he says, we have the brain of a mass murderer, the purest incarnation of evil ever to walk among us. A man of indeterminate race. His skin more sheen than pigment. They say light deflected off of him, wanted no part of him. He slaughtered country folk, city folk, women and children, old and young. He slit the throat of any woman who resembled his mother, and yes he slit hers too. This lump of matter soaking in formaldehyde is the engine that kept him killing. It's been photographed and microscoped in every civilized city on this globe. The findings? Identical to yours and mine in all respects. Why, then, do we exhibit it? A reminder, ladies and gentlemen. There are things ordained by God that science cannot explain away.

Looks like a cow's brain, someone says.

People laugh, but the boy just stares ahead.

Son, the professor answers, this establishment employs the finest scientific minds. Surely they are capable of distinguishing between organs belonging to livestock and those belonging to human beings.

He leads us to the next exhibit. The lights dim, then rise again on a moss-haired girl with painted hands. The men all cluck their tongues. She's sitting cross-legged, smoking a water pipe, wearing a tight corset and a garter with beaded fringe. Drumming plays on a phonograph behind the backcloth. The cloth itself features palm trees and eastern-looking facades, the kind with doorways cut like keyholes.

This, ladies and gentlemen, is our own Circassian Serpent Queen. A woman of the world's purest Caucasian stock, stolen during a Turkish raid and sold in the white slave markets of Constantinople. After five long years in the seraglio of a Persian sultan, one of our agents, at great peril to his own life, was able to liberate her from her depraved servitude. Aboard ship it was discovered that she had a peculiar talent, which she shall demonstrate for you now.

The Queen rocks her hips and ripples her arms, her bracelets clanking like cymbals at the base of her wrists. A speckled snake sticks its head out of her hair, surveys the audience as though it's counting the house. People in front step back. Only the boy holds his ground.

A king cobra, the lecturer says. The most temperamental of all venomous serpents.

He prods the snake's head with the tip of his pointer. Its hood flares out, its jaws snap open. A sound like growling breaks from its throat.

Note the ribs in the neck, the professor says. The saliva gathering at the fangs. The cobra's poison saps the nervous system, causes blindness, dizziness, death. Watch how our Beauty tames it.

The snake rises vertically from her hair, angles back, then lunges forward, striking at the space between us. The Queen begins cooing—a low hum in time to the drums. The snake relaxes its hood, starts to sway. The Queen lifts a hand to its chin. Slowly, the cobra rests its head on her wrist, winds its body down her bare arm. The professor leads the audience in applause.

A succession of snakes part her hair, the professor naming them as they appear—puff adder, black racer, spotted rock python. By the time the Queen stands to take her bow, her arms and legs are braided in snakes. There's a constrictor wound around her belly, a crossbanded viper covering her neck like a scarf. Men whistle as the lights dim.

The Queen is followed by Siamese twins joined at the buttocks, a man with a third arm jutting out of his chest, a seven-foot Chinaman, a woman so fat she occupies two exhibit spaces.

Now, the professor says, for our star oddity.

We're standing in front of what looks like a large box draped in baize. The surrounding scrims are covered with happy farm scenes—morning sun shining on barn, silo, corn and farmer. A staccato snorting comes from under the cloth. The professor tugs the fabric free, revealing a four-hoofed creature stalled in a makeshift sty, it's face human, its body a pig's. The sty is enclosed in a metal cage, the animal chained by the neck to a pole, its back legs trussed together.

This horror of crossbreeding, the professor says, is the pride of our hall. Notice the shoat-like nose, the lack of jointure where the elbows and knees should be. We found him wallowing in a Florida swamp, half starved to death. Part human, part pig.

Which part birthed and abandoned him, we'd rather not specu-late. We call him our Porcine Child. If he's part human, you might ask, then why not favor that part? Well ladies and gentle-men, we tried it that way, but the creature would not cooperate. Metal is the only substance it won't chew through. No amount of training could convince it that a toilet was for anything but drinking. What's more, linguists from seven of our nation's top universities found no way to communicate with it. No, the poor beast—the only one of its kind—is as ill-suited for society as it is for the wild. Here, at least, the price of admission keeps it fed and cared for.

The professor stands back, gestures for us to surround the cage. The pig-creature moves as close to the bars as the chain will allow, its purple tongue flicking out from between human lips, its nostrils flaring. I stick with the boy as he circles the sty. The creature's hoofs are sutured to its skin, the stub-tail some kind of spinal deformity. His pink body is shaved smooth, bloat-ed—a dwarf rather than a boy. Impossible to know if this was his design or someone else's—if he hired the man who hacked off his hands and feet, or was tied down as a child. A college kid bangs on top of the cage with his fists. His friend dips a piece of licorice between the bars, jerks it away when the dwarf lunges. The professor grins.

We finish our tour and wait. The boy slides a penny into a mechanized trough, feeds the creature crumbled hardtack from his cupped palms. There's nothing on the boy's face to say if he's feeding it out of pity or if he wants to see what it looks like when it eats. Either way, he should know better. This is the wrong kind of spectacle, its only purpose to keep a crowd going. No different than my days on the medicine trail, when I played the cigar-store Indian who came to life, juggling tomahawks and hollering war chants. Once enough people had gathered, Connor would sell them his medicine—homemade prune and sugar water, 80 proof. He claimed there was nothing it couldn't cure.

The professor is barking us on to the wax works collection, but I turn around, exit the way we came. I wait for a while under the museum's awning, squinting the light from my eyes. There's a man on the opposite sidewalk, standing with his hands in his coat pockets, stretching his neck from side to side. I see him watching me, then notice that I'm standing with my hand and hook in my coat pockets, stretching my neck from side to side. I can't make out his face, but I recognize the slumping shoulders, the hunched spine. It's Jonson, dressed in a duster and a tan slicker, smiling at me through gaps in the traffic. I step to the curb, wait for the cars to clear. But before I can cross he's turned the corner and is gone.

• • •

In the hotel, I open my valise, press on a bump in the fabric that releases the false backing. The bottom row of hooks rises, exposing two envelopes, a pencil, an eraser, a small pad of paper. I put the money that isn't mine in one envelope, the money that is in the other. Sitting with my back to the bed, I empty the second envelope across my lap, count the bills, subtract their total from the tailor's price. The numbers are close—a few more towns, a few more cities, and they will be the same.

I take up the pad, flip through the pages. Each page is drawn over with the outline of a man's suit. I've filled the torsos with circles, stars, squares—the circles standing in for sapphires, the stars for rhinestones, the squares for rubies. On one suit I've drawn circle-studded stripes down each sleeve, on another I've dotted the arms with squares and stars. I've penciled in rhinestone collars, ruby collars, mixed collars. Some of the torsos I've covered with distinct shapes—the bulb and stem of a rose over each breast pocket; stick-figure fish swimming vertically, horizontally; small birds in various stages of flight. Others I've filled with patterns—checkered rhinestones, wavy lines of sapphires, ruby pinstripes.

I turn through the pages, pencil in hand, erase a half-circle of squares from one torso, add a line of stars to another. With each addition or deletion I imagine the changing pattern of light. I close my eyes, place myself in the audience, squint at the reflection from the front row, the back row.

I snap the false backing shut, empty the insides of my prosthetics onto the bed. I divide the contents into two rows, one for vials with a single notch carved into the stopper, the other for vials with two notches. Each notch stands for a time I've skimmed. It's early in the run, but already the double-notched vials outnumber the single-notched vials. I've never sold a triple-notched vial.

I tell myself I'll conserve. I'll take smaller and smaller tastes, until I'm cutting half-notches in the stoppers, until I'm able to go several days without carving any notches at all.

I pack away the prosthetics, leave one single-notched vial on the bed.

Chicago to Sioux City, Iowa

September 8, 1922

The night train is quiet. I have a compartment to myself. It's rare to get a full bench, but now I have two, facing each other, and a door to block the sounds of people moving past. I stack my luggage overhead, cover a bench with a pillow and blanket. Before I've closed my eyes, the door jolts open, and Jonson's standing there silhouetted by the hall light.

Thought you might like some company, he says, holding out a bottle.

I was asleep, I say.

To hell you were. Can't nobody but my boy sleep on these things, and that's only 'cause he was raised on them.

Neither of us mentions the museum.

Listen, he says, I come in friendship. We started on the wrong foot.

I didn't think we were on any foot at all.

You can play it that way, he says. I'm trying to make things right.

He sits on the blanket at my feet. I pivot, press my back straight against the bench. Jonson's ogling my hacked arm.

Ain't seen the stump before, he says.

No need to cover it when I'm sleeping.

Might lose an eye, he observes.

I lean forward, pull my prosthetic from where I'd wedged it between two suitcases. Jonson watches me work in my stump, smiling. A number of his top teeth are gone.

He screws off the cap, hands me the bottle. Even as I put the mouth to my lips, I know he wants something in return.

I heard you done that yourself, he says.

Done what? I say, passing him the bottle. He taps his wrist, gestures like he's sawing.

Why would I've done that?

There's a juggler on every bill, he says. Ain't but one with his hand cut off.

I don't say anything. The compartment's lit by a weak bulb, the window black save the occasional flicker from a gantry crane or farmhouse porch. I shut my eyes, feel myself warm to the whiskey.

Ain't you had enough? Jonson asks.

Of what?

Split weeks and sleeper jumps. Dickering over your slot on the bill. How old are you, Swain?

Old enough.

I'd say older than that. What's going to happen for you that ain't already happened? Maybe it's time to say die.

And do what?

He pulls his grouch bag from under his shirt, takes out a vial and lifts it into the light coming through the compartment door. The vial is filled with silver-blue liquid. Jonson watches me close.

Thought you was careful? he says.

I look him up and down. I hadn't seen the signs, but Jonson, all gums and jaundice, had seen it in me. It's clear now what his boy was doing in that store.

He balances the bottle between his knees, pulls the stopper from the vial. Using one hand to steady the other, he lets two drops fall into the whiskey.

I'll fill this up later, he says, replacing the stopper, tucking the vial into his shirt pocket.

Business must be good, I say. Two of us working the same bill.

Must be.

He swells his cheeks with whiskey, holds the liquor in his mouth until his eyes start to glow.

Let it seep in, he says, passing me the bottle. I don't hesitate.

Truth is, he says, we do them good by skimming. The more we skim, the more people got to buy.

It burns my throat, cuts into my chest from the inside. Jonson takes away the bottle.

You'll be fine in a minute, he says. Whiskey makes it all go faster.

He's right about that much. The pain is gone as quick as it came. Specks of blue break through my vision.

How long they got you for? he asks.

A while.

And then? You think the circuit will keep you on?

I'm not worried.

Cream don't always rise.

What does that mean?

Means you'll want to keep the right people happy.

Is that a warning?

Advice.

Yours, or someone else's?

It's worth heeding either way. Your second profession might end up your first.

He pulls a rolled cigarette from his shirt pocket, holds it between his lips and strikes a match against the heel of his shoe. He keeps striking until the match lights. He does all of this one-handed.

How was that? he asks.

I breathe in the smoke, slump my head against the bench. There's no pain anywhere in me.

Tell me something, he says. Why'd you take that first taste?

He's timed it right. The part of me that knows to stay quiet is undone.

All right, I say. I did a turn at the Majestic once.

Like hell.

I wasn't much older than your boy is now. Back then I had a slack wire act. Juggling was the smallest part of what I did.

It ain't easy to picture, Jonson says. Not now.

Have you ever walked a wire?

You ever danced on a barrel?

Most people bow out before they take the first step. They get to the top of the platform and that's it. It's like being on a horse that bucks. Once it knows you're afraid, you'll never ride that horse again.

I'll bet you didn't scare.

No, I didn't. I had a turn with a unicycle. I'd ride back and forth from one platform to the other. The first time it was simple coasting. The second time I'd be blindfolded. The third, blindfolded and juggling. The fourth blindfolded, juggling, and pedaling backwards. I'd get house boys to shake the platforms. The trombone would play notes that sounded like falling, but I never fell.

Sounds better than what you got now.

It was no shut act.

So why are you here with me?

I don't know.

You know.

All right, I say. I know.

Any chance you'll share?

You first, I say.

I reach out my hand and he gives up the bottle. It's a good while before I pass it back.

Some performers can see their act play out in their mind, I say. For them it's as good as done on the boards. Others can see up to a point before their minds stick. Maybe they freeze at the final flip. Maybe they hear the punch line but not the laughter. Your boy is the first type. I used to be.

You took a spill?

Yeah.

Bad?

Bad enough.

Might have been a one-time thing.

It wasn't.

Let me guess, he says. A taste from the vials and you can see any damn thing you like?

Uh-huh.

Just not when it counts.

No. But it feels right at the time.

He smiles. Maybe we need a little more, he says, taking the vial back out of his pocket. When he's done he hands the bottle over. For a while he lets us sit in quiet. I hunch forward, listening to the train's gears. Soon I'm at the Majestic, my scalp slick under the calcium spot. I rise up on the pedals, spread my palm over the seat, lift myself into a handstand, a good ten feet off the stage. I stay balanced like that, buttressed by the applause. I'm about to dismount with a flip when Jonson whistles in my ear. He slides his hand up my shoulder, closes it around my throat. Before I have my balance, he's straddling my body, pinning my prosthetic down. The applause stop short.

Listen you dumb son of a bitch, he says. I want you

thinking on this while that shit settles in—stay clear of my boy. You hear me? Stay away.

He tightens his grip. I do what I can to nod.

That works for us both, he says.

In the morning, the conductor finds me lying on the floor between the benches, my face hidden in the crook of my good arm.

Marion, California

May 1902

We arrived in town early on a weekend morning. I sat on the back flap of Connor's covered wagon, the balls of my feet brushing the ground while he drove the main street. At each corner I hopped off, pitched a double-sided placard with the same message painted on either side: FOLLOW THE CLARION CALL AND BE CURED.

We parked in a stone-walled square, set a card table before the fountain, weighted the table legs with medicine bags, covered the top with a paisley cloth and lined rows of bottles on either side of a signboard listing the ailments Connor's brew could cure. The last entry read, MANY, MANY MORE.

I changed in the back of the wagon while Connor readied his voice, repeating the same nonce word up and down the scale, stretching his jaws wide and pushing out his tongue. My costume was thick for summer, the deerskin sleeves taut at the elbows, the moccasins too small. I coated my hands, face, and neck with a deep-red base, added black and white war-stripes beneath my eyes, applied a light powder to keep the base from melting. I fitted tomahawks into loops along the belt, pulled on a feathered headdress and tied the strap beneath my chin.

By mid-morning the sky was starting to brighten, the air to warm. Connor fetched his bugle from the jockey box, gestured for me to take my place beside the table. I stood with my arms stiff at my sides, a tomahawk locked in each fist, feathers dangling from the handles.

Remember, Connor said. Just keep your eyes fixed on a spot in the distance. Nothing to it.

The hawkers, carters and vagrants who frequented the square were the first to gather round. Then came clerks, construction workers, boys who'd been playing stickball in a nearby alley, tourists and retirees, the sick and lame. The square filled. People raised up on tiptoes, stood on the stone coping surrounding the fountain. Connor set aside his trumpet, addressed the crowd.

Ladies and gentlemen, he started, what I offer you today is a cure-all discovered by my grandfather, refined by my father, and further refined by me. An ancestral brew known to cure the sick and bolster the strong. I would be betraying my ancestors' memory were I to name the ingredients, but I can say this: the components are pure and the formula patented. I carry the patent with me should you need convincing. This is no potion, and I am no alchemist. What's more, should it fail to treat your ills, simply keep the empty bottle and when I return this way in a month's time, I will refund your money, every cent.

How about you come back in a month and if it worked we pay you then?

I'm a patient man, Connor said. But not that patient.

What does it do, exactly?

A fine question, Connor said. A very good question indeed. When I said it was a cure-all, I meant just that. Allow me to provide an example. A woman, a school teacher, told me she'd never gone a day in her life without an ache or a pain of some kind—a stiff back, a bum knee, a sore tooth, a strained neck, and any other discomfort you might name. A migraine every evening and nausea the next morning. She bought a bottle, figuring she had nothing to lose. Well, when I came back around just one month later, she was waiting for me, eager to purchase the next month's supply. Another woman, a widow, told me she could not sleep, could not so much as shut her eyes without seeing her husband as he appeared in the final, agonizing moments of his life. Well, one tablespoon and not only was she able to sleep, but she could see her beloved again as he was on the day they met: young and strong, with color in his cheeks, the hero of her youth. If you doubt me, I have their written testimonies, along with many others, in my possession. Long term, this fortifying brew has been known to cure microcephalis, quinsy, rachitis, cleptomania, and diptheria, to name a few. It's been known to shrink benign and malignant tumors alike. It purges the system of parasites, thickens thinning blood, and clears skin of boils and other blemishes. It has repeatedly healed where all other remedies have failed. I have seen it cure husbands of their lust and wives of their frigidity. It provides the weary with stamina, the fearful with courage. A mere teaspoon has produced a sustained bout of studying in the most undisciplined of children. At a dollar a bottle you have everything to gain, and what's more, I will discount the price by a percentage of ten for the first five patrons. A ninety-cent investment in your health and well-being.

Is there anything it can't do?

It cannot bring the dead back to life, make the old young, the poor rich, or the talentless talented. Apart from that, I have yet to discover its limitations.

A man stepped forward, held up a knurled hand, the tips of the fingers forking backward at the joint.

Arthritis, the man said. Got so my hand's no better than a paper weight.

An awful predicament, Connor said. I suffered from a similar affliction, only in my toes. It was this very recipe that cured me. Tell me, sir, have you any hobbies?

I write poems.

Professionally?

Wouldn't be a hobby if I did it professionally.

I mean have you published.

No sir. I handpick the people I share them with.

A wise practice. Tell me, can you make a fist?

What you see is what you get.

And is that the hand you write with?

It was. I do my writing in my head now.

Like Homer.

OK.

Well, let's see if we can't get your verse from head to paper.

Connor crouched down, took up a bottle, wrote directions on the label while he spoke.

A teaspoon at breakfast, another at dinner, he instructed. If you want to accelerate the healing process, I'd recommend you rub a cotton swab's worth on each knuckle before bed. Allow the medicine to soak directly into the bone and you'll see a difference when you wake.

The odor won't keep me up nights?

Quite the contrary. It's dulcet scent will work on you much like a lullaby.

And that's ninety cents?

Ninety cents for the first five purchasers. Now, for a man whose condition is in such advanced stages, I'd recommend two, possibly three bottles.

Like you said, I got nothing to lose.

People began to queue up. There was a pregnant woman who'd miscarried twice before, a man who'd had the same case of hives for more than a year, another man who'd just turned thirty though his skin was wrinkled and his hair gray. When the people on line outnumbered the people in the crowd Connor gestured toward me, said:

Ladies and gentlemen, now for a bit of native entertainment.

I broke my pose, lunged forward, hollering war cries and hurling tomahawks. Children darted behind their parents, began inching back out.

Don't be afraid, Connor said. He's quite tame. I liberated him from his depraved existence on an Apache reservation outside of Tulsa, Oklahoma. His father rode with Geronimo. A proud people living in squalor. This one calls himself Wet River. His name is all the language he knows.

Connor stood watching as I edged off to the side, bringing the children and some parents with me, then returned to his patients, diagnosing their conditions, prescribing doses, scribbling on labels.

I balanced a tomahawk on my nose, juggled others behind my back, then passed them between my legs. Counterfeit weapons, the stone a clay-painted foam. Connor bought them at a penny a piece from a theater that was shutting its doors. I finished my first set, took a slight bow with my shoulders. A small, tow-headed child asked if he could try. His mother tugged him away.

Connor's plan was working. The sideshow held the crowd. The crowd itself drew more people. We'd been playing for hours before the square cleared.

• • •

I've never had a better day, Connor said once we'd quit the town. Never in all my years. You did a fine job, son. A fine, fine job.

He drew back on the reins, looked up and down the roadway as though people might be watching from behind the pepper trees.

By God, I'd believe you were pure native, he said. Even at this distance. Damned authentic.

He slapped at the horse to quicken its pace, drove on.

You think you've failed, but you haven't. No one is a failure because of a single fall.

I know.

No, you don't. People have it wrong: yours is the oldest profession. There were jugglers on the streets of Jericho and in the Forum at Rome, in the stalls of Aztec and Assyrian marketplaces, in the courts of European monarchs and Arabian caliphs. The costumes and objects may change with time, but the juggler has always been with us, and always will be. Do you understand me?

I think so.

Let me put it this way: You were right in refusing to speak. I didn't understand, but now I do. You tap into an essential mystery. You stand out of time, a figure from the past and present and future, a fixed point in the full sweep of history. Nobody knows why you do what you do, no more than they know why they watch. You move people from a mundane plane of existence to a sphere beyond the everyday. As they stand there watching you, they cease to be clerks, dentists, lawyers, politicians, vagabonds, thieves. They are not thinking about how to pay the rent or when they are going to die. There is only the mesmeric whirl. You meet a fundamental need, a need as fundamental as food or sex. You put a stop to the mind's ceaseless chatter, if only for a moment. I want you to consider that.

OK.

Promise me.

I promise.

All right, he said. Now, let's celebrate the day's fortune.

He pulled a bottle of medicine from his blazer pocket, uncorked it with his teeth, spit the cork onto the road. We passed the bottle back and forth, taking short drags, then long swallows. We'd emptied a third bottle before we made camp. When I woke the next morning, my face was still painted, the head-dress still strapped beneath my chin.

Sioux City, Iowa

September 9, 1922

Everything in and surrounding the town is flat, sheered fields on one side of the tracks, squat buildings on the other. A few yards up the platform Jonson and his boy are fussing with their luggage. I watch them fasten their barrels to a dolly, strap their bindles to their backs. Jonson sees me watching, smiles. He waves me over, but I stay back, wait for them to trundle their barrels away. I feel the whiskey thinning in my blood.

I find a coffee shop on my way to the theater. The inside is meant to look rustic, the floor and ceiling made of the same light-grained wood, the walls decorated with paint-by-numbers of waterfalls, forests, native-Indian faces. The place is empty except for a wall-eyed kid at the counter who keeps staring at my trunk. He's a shine, the type who wants to talk his way onstage. I take the booth nearest the door, sit with my back to him, my trunk propped on the opposite bench.

A man in an apron jots down my order. I roll my neck, shut my eyes. My tongue's furring over and my gut's churning. I think in pictures, everything right on top of me, blotting out whatever's behind. The Porcine Child nodding off a snarl of flies. Jonson spraying saliva through the gaps in his teeth. I pinch the flap of my ear, dig my nails in.

The kid waits for my food to arrive. A shine trick—now I'm

stuck for as long as it takes me to eat. I watch his shadow spread over the table.

Excuse me, mister? he says.

It's sir.

What?

When you're talking to someone you never met before it's sir. Mister is an insult.

I didn't mean it to be, he says. Then adds, You here for the shows?

He's got a canvas glove hanging from each back pocket and his frame barely fills his clothes. He looks like a kid who's used to being barked at.

Can I sit? he asks.

I'm in a hurry.

I won't take a minute.

Not today, son.

I start cutting up my flapjacks. The kid clears his throat.

Did you hear the one about the widower who married his wife's sister?

What?

He didn't want to break in a new mother-in-law.

I don't say anything.

I write jokes, he says. For sale.

I have a dumb act.

What?

I don't talk onstage. I juggle.

But you could, he says. People sing while they play the piano. You could tell jokes while you juggle.

I'm not interested.

But you know people.

They aren't interested either.

He straightens his spine.

Did you hear the one about the southern planter? he says. He was an undertaker from New Orleans.

That's enough, kid, I say.

I stand, step from the booth. He digs his fingers into his thighs. His smile gives out.

Fine, he says. That's fine.

He starts to leave, then turns back.

You know, he says, a year ago our theater was a butcher's shop. You're shit if they sent you here, mister.

He makes a show of slamming the door. The counter-man laughs. I look over my shoulder. He's sitting on a stool, stropping a ladle against the skirt of his apron.

Kid's half scrambled, he says. But he speaks his mind. Gotta give him that.

I do, I say.

The flapjacks are swelling in my stomach, soaking in the whiskey. Bits of undone batter clog my throat. I look back at the man in the apron. He sees it in me.

That way, he says, pointing with his ladle.

I sprint the distance from the back stoop to the outhouse, a clapboard box with a hole in the door where the knob should be. I loop in two fingers, pull, feel a thick splinter break my skin. My head spikes back at the stench. After a while, my stomach settles, my skin cools. I stand, pull the splinter free with my teeth.

I order a second pot of coffee, empty cup after cup until my mind clears. On my walk to the theater I see the shine loading sacks of feed onto a flatbed truck, his back sloping under the weight.

• • •

The performer's entrance is off a gravel side alley. A houseboy with a gumboil on his chin greets me at the door, tells me I'll be dressing in the cellar.

I stop at the notice board. Beneath the hell-and-damn edict there's a telegram with my name on it:

> Two weeks since I heard from you. Following address good for ten days: 20 S. Maple, #4, Ogden, N.Y.

I'm to deliver ten vials to 5 N. Ogden Street between two and four in the afternoon. If there was a message for Jonson he'd already found it. He'd likely found mine, too. I tear the scrap of paper free of its tack, fold it into my coat pocket.

The basement hallway cuts through six dressing stalls, four on one side, two on the other. I hear the contortionist playing his ocarina, two sisters from the sister act bickering in their stage voices. There are remnants of a butcher's shop cluttered against the back of my stall—reams of meat paper, jars of brine and marinade, a rusted sausage stuffer, pairs of mesh gloves, the hook from a hanging scale. There's a mirror with no frame nailed to the wall beside the door, a folding table and chair set up underneath. No wash basin, no towel.

I uncordon my valises, hang a linen cloth from the nail on the opposite wall, hang my stage suit up against the cloth. I dig out a small bag of make-up, sit at the mirror. The folds of skin beneath my eyes look like burst water blisters. I cover them over with burnt cork, change into my costume, count the rounds of applause until it's my turn to take the stage.

I'm debuting something new in my act, something I've saved to try out on a smaller market. I've bolted metal loops into the striped balls, taught myself to catch and throw by spearing the loops with my hook. I've got six balls going, my good hand buried in my pants pocket. It's working. I get applause, a few whistles. I move to the edge of the stage, toss the balls like they're headed for the third row, reel them back. The trick is to get enough spin. People in the front throw up their hands, then laugh. I step back, the balls still turning, take a blindfold from my pocket, slip it over my eyes. My hook finds the loop every time.

There's a shout, and I hear seats emptying, boots clumping up the aisles. The balls bounce around my ankles. By the time I get my blindfold off the audience is down to three crag-faced women near the back. The one in the middle is smiling, looking sad or maybe simple. I gather up the striped balls, get a wide circle going. I take it slow until my arms quit shaking.

I'm ready to bow off when the doors open and people start filing back in. They're talking amongst themselves, excited, but by the time they're sitting again they've gone quiet. I pick the blindfold up from where I'd dropped it.

When it's over, Jonson's waiting for me in the wings.

You got one-upped by a mule, he says.

What?

A runaway mule. Rabid. Bucking and screaming. It kicked out the bank window. Took half the town to get it calm.

I raise my shoulders.

They came back, I say.

• • •

Downstairs, I open my valise, take up the prosthetics one by one, slide the vials from the hollows and line them in rows on the table. I select five single-notched vials, five double-notched vials, return the rest to their sockets. I change out of my costume, wipe the cork from under my eyes.

The map leads me to a store-lined boulevard in an otherwise residential neighborhood—a red-brick facade set between

a bookshop and a grocer's, a street lifted from a larger city. A
copper plaque beside the door gives a company name, but there's
nothing to say what the company does. I ring the buzzer, survey
the block while I wait. There's an open fire plug flooding the
gutter, crows drinking from the run off. The sidewalks and cars
are empty. The door opens behind me. I turn, find myself looking over the shoulder of a man half my weight and into a long,
narrow loft.

The buyer extends his right, then his left hand.

Please, come in, he says.

I glance back, step inside. The sun is bright and at first the
objects on the walls are blacked out behind a spread of purple. I
follow him to a small, square table at the center of the store. My
vision clears, and I see weapons mounted like works of art with
plates underneath telling where they're from and how much
they cost. There's one that looks like the top of a child-sized
pitchfork, the prongs close together, the silver pure and polished; there's a sword sheathed in a hard-leather case, pennons
dangling from the handle, jewels covering the stitching; there's
a musket from the Civil War or earlier, its mouth spread open
like a trumpet, its trigger curled and long like a half-bent finger.

You know, he says, sitting, I've never thought of the prosthetic as a weapon, but it would serve.

He leans across, runs a finger along the slight curve of my
hook, makes a sound like purring. He's dressed in a black sack
suit, his tie tugged loose at the collar, the underflap tucked into
his breast pocket. His face is jowly, his skin mottled. He's slapped
himself up and down with cologne, but his clothes stink of dope.

May I see it? he asks.

I start lifting the vials from my pockets.

No, no, he says, pointing at my hook.

The stump?

Stump is a vulgar word.

Why do you want to see it?

For the same reason I collect rare weapons, he says. They are objects of beauty and elegance, yet their purpose is to inflict trauma on the body. Shouldn't that trauma also be beautiful, elegant?

I don't have much time, I say.

A quick look.

I tug my stump from the hollow, set the hook on the table. I start to peel the stub sock free, but he holds up a hand.

Please, he says, reaching across. He works his index fingers under the soft-cotton gauze on either side of my forearm, inches the sock forward, inspects each bit of unveiled skin.

Shoddy, he says, clucking his tongue. A saw, was it?

A drawknife.

Serrated?

Yes.

He runs his thumb over the rucked skin, taps the cauliflower nub.

Neuroma, he says. A nerve ending that was not properly severed. Does it press against the prosthetic?

Yes.

It must cause you some discomfort. Who did this to you?

It doesn't matter.

Not a surgeon?

No.

I wouldn't think so.

He smiles. Well, he says, now for business.

I pull on the sock, the prosthetic, set the vials on the table and name the price.

I need a taste first, he says. I need to know that what I'm buying and what I ordered are the same.

They're the same, I say.

I must be sure.

He takes a handkerchief from his breast pocket, drapes it over his index finger, picks up a vial with two notches carved into the stopper. He touches the liquid to the fabric, holds his finger to the gum just above his front tooth. It won't take long for him to know—the spot he's touched will turn warm, start to burn. The farther the burning spreads, the stronger the product. I wait. His jaws knot up, then fall open.

It's been better, he says. But, yes, this will do. He gathers up the vials with one hand, reaches into his pocket with the other.

I trust you'll find your own way out, he says.

I leave him with his head hanging limp, saliva purling out the corners of his mouth.

• • •

A pain in my gut stops me from going on. I buckle in the wings, lie on my side. People are murmuring around me. I hear soft applause coming from the crowd. I'm lifted to my feet, guided to a couch in a back room. The manager sets a bucket on the floor in front of me. I wait, but no doctor shows. The cushions under me turn damp with sweat.

I focus my eyes on the cracks in the ceiling, stare them down until they stop squirming. After a while, my stomach settles, my skin cools. I decide I'll stay where I am until someone comes for me.

The someone who comes is Jonson, still spotted with the powder he wears onstage. He looks around the room. I look with him. The walls curve up into the ceiling like the back side of a cave. The wood floors are unsanded, unvarnished. Besides the couch I'm sitting on there's a pile of kindling, a lidless garbage can filled with towels, an assortment of tools lying loose on a wood bench. Pictures of dime-store performers stand upside down and sideways against two of the four walls.

This would work nice, Jonson says, sitting next to me. Ever wonder why you can't just find yourself a little room like this?

No, I say.

Sure you do, he says. A man wants to be left alone or he don't want nothing.

Then why are you here?

He smiles. Came to see how you're doing.

I'll live.

But for how long?

I stop myself from asking what he means. He pats my knee, stands.

I bet you was scared with all those weapons on the walls, he says.

I keep my face calm.

Why not tell me what you want? I ask.

That's a good question, he says. Someone's paying me. It's up to you to figure out who. I will tell you this—warning you ain't in my job description. I'm looking out for you, Swain.

He pauses in the doorway, switches off the light.

Might be you think better in the dark, he says.

• • •

It's late when I get to the hotel. The bed posts are covered with thick clots of dust, the wall opposite my bed is paneled with mirrors. I cross the room, open the window, pull the curtain shut. The remaining vials are spread over my blanket. All but a few are double-notched, with more than a week before I reach the new supply. I kneel in front of the mattress, pick up a single-notched vial, roll it back and forth in my palm. Small shards of silver disperse into the blue, then regroup.

I slide my travel bag out from under the bed, untie the drawstring, push aside my socks, my underclothes, a tennis ball, a small book of newspaper clippings dating to my first days onstage. There are Canadian coins and bits of pocket lint resting on the bottom. I find a double-sided cotton swab—one side dirty, one side clean—rest it on my thigh, thumb the stopper from the vial. I stand the vial in front of me, work the clean tip through its open mouth. I hold the colored cotton under my tongue. The burn gives way to a rush of saliva.

Lying on my back, I feel a humming so slight I doubt it's real. I squeeze my eyes shut, trace the liquid's path to my brain, trying to push it deeper. My elbows and knees spasm, go rigid. Then nothing.

• • •

Next morning, Jonson and his boy are standing a few feet away on the platform, Jonson smoking a cigarette that won't stay lit, the boy leaning against his barrel, singing softly to himself. The train is delayed; no one will say for how long. The rain comes and goes. Jonson flicks his cigarette onto the tracks, starts toward me.

You look like shit, he says. Even for a cripple.

His eyes are yellow beneath the pupils, his jaw line spotted with swollen pimples.

I got something to tell you, he says.

Yeah?

He starts rolling a second cigarette. He hunches over the paper, holds the tobacco close to his chest. His back looks near breaking; his arms are all bone, his stomach bloated. He's been reduced to shuffling in his act—nothing but a steady beat for the boy.

A man came to see me, he says. About my son.

A man?

A browser. All the way from New York City.

About the boy?

None other.

What did he want?

Said he had a part only my boy could play.

In New York?

On a street I figure you heard of.

No surprise, I say. Like you said, the boy's got talent.

True, but talent will keep. He ain't ready. Not yet.

He might be.

You mean the way you was ready?

He walks back to where he'd been standing. The boy doesn't seem to notice that he's returned or that he'd ever gone. Jonson flicks his cigarette onto the tracks.

Cut that singing, he says. I hear the train.

I understand now why he keeps his son tied to a hinterland circuit. Watching them gather their gear as the train arrives, I start to imagine two lives for the boy: one with his father, and one without.

Osgood, Indiana

September 15, 1922

I walk down wide residential streets, cut through a park, come out in a neighborhood that's been stripped bare and abandoned, all squat brick shells and broken glass. The cash in my pocket rubs against my thigh. I'm beginning to feel as if I'll never get there, as if I'm walking in place, passing the same damaged facade, the same busted bicycle again and again. I quicken my stride, start to run.

There's no sign naming the shop, just a number painted in black on the brick beside a tin mailbox. I ring the bell and the door opens inward. The old man has trouble getting out of its way. He's dressed in sockfeet and frayed pajamas. Liver spots cover the backs of his hands, shade the peaks in his hairline.

Please enter, Mr. Swain.

I'm sorry to wake you.

Not at all.

Inside, the only light comes from a dim lamp clamped to a drafting table. A burlap scrim cuts the room in two.

Wait here while I fetch it, he says.

I watch him walk away, his heels rising off the ground, exposing the black bottoms of his white socks. He parts the curtain, lets it fall shut behind him. The front room is crowded with objects of his trade—a sewing machine with a cracked treadle, a mannequin torso dressed in lace jabot, teetering stacks of mismatched cloth. Near the center of the floor there's a heap of dust that he'd swept into a mound but hadn't bothered to discard. There are no family portraits, no upholstered chairs, no magazines or toys. The room smells like months of the old man's breath and sweat.

I've found it, he calls through the curtain. Get yourself ready.

I unbutton my shirt, unbuckle my belt, remove my hook and strip to my underclothes.

This is it, Mr. Swain, he says, backing his way through the burlap. I trust you will be pleased.

He flicks on the overhead light, raises the suit to his chin. It's studded with counterfeit gems, the fabric white, blue stripes sewn down the sleeves, glitter glued over every stitch. The collar is lined with rhinestones, the right sleeve wider than the left.

Please, he says. Try it on.

He wheels a mirror to the center of the room while I dress. I bend my knees, roll my shoulders, feel the fabric start to conform to my body. The tailor is grinning, applauding his own work. I slip my stump back in the socket. He takes my shoulders, turns me toward the mirror.

Every bit of me shines. Onstage, under the calcium spot, with sparkles stickered to the balls, I'll look like fireworks exploding up a blind alley.

• • •

Jonson's rolling his barrel offstage as I walk on. He claps his lips together, then whistles through the gaps in his teeth. The lights go down; a single beam spots me from top to bottom.

I start my routine, but something's not right. The balls seem far away. I feel myself reaching for them. I move closer, deepen the bend in my arms. My eyes strain, maybe from the single light and the surrounding dark, maybe from the glint off the gems.

I make it through the first set, move to the edge of the stage, throw the balls up, hide my good hand behind my back. My hook spears loop after loop. I'm feeling steadier; faces in the front row seem to be smiling. One woman holds up her hands, fingers splayed, shielding herself.

I'm nearing the end but decide to keep going. I squat down, start the balls spinning faster. I hear people whispering. Everything is happening almost without me. But then one of the rhinestone cufflinks catches the light, deflects it in a sharp line that finds my eye. I jerk my head away, feel my hook scrape against the surface of a ball, watch the ball spin toward the audience, picking up speed in the air. It strikes the shin of an old woman in the front row, doubles her out of her seat. The audience stands as I back into the wings.

The manager fines me twice what I paid for the suit.

• • •

I'm feeling for the rag in my pocket when Jonson rattles my door.

Swainee, he says. I know you're in there. You got nowhere else to be.

I swipe the vials under my pillow, pull the covers up the bed.

A minute, I say.

That's right, he says. Make yourself decent.

I open the door; he doesn't wait for me to invite him inside.

Want to talk some business, he says.

Yeah?

Come to make you an offer—discreet like. I got some you can buy.

How's that?

Had a cancellation. They told me to find my own buyer.

I don't say anything.

Listen, Jonson says, I'll cut you a deal. That suit-a-stones for three vials.

What would you do with it?

I like my pajamas with rocks on them. What do you care? You ain't going to wear it no more. Unless crippling the audience is part of your act now.

Not interested, I say.

You ain't been doing so well lately, he says. I'm trying to help you out.

I'll be all right.

To hell you will. Take my offer.

No, thank you.

You got something going I don't know about?

No.

Well you best find something. I'm done being cute with you. Them rocks didn't work. Cutting off your hand didn't work. Truth is, you only got one way to keep alive. Think on it, Swain. Think real quick.

When he's gone, I replace the vials in the hollows of my prosthetics, link the chain through the handles, lock the padlock and pocket the key. I work the bed against the wall with my knees, stretch the suit out on the floor, smooth down the wrinkles with my palm. I fold the legs over the torso, the sleeves over the legs, careful to leave slack at the bends so the fabric won't crease. I tape the suit back up in the tailor's brown wrapping, hurry outside.

The wide residential streets have gone quiet. A sign says the park closes at dusk, but there's nothing to keep me from walking through. The main path is lined with trees whose leaves are just starting to fall. I stray from the pavement in the dark, stumble over cracks in the asphalt. I walk fast, sucking in all the breath my chest will hold.

There's a light flickering beneath the drape in the tailor's window. Across the street, a cluster of hobos shamble around a tin ash can, burning what smells like rubber and driftwood. Their frayed dusters and porous bowlers glow white.

The tailor opens his door as far as the chain will allow.

This is no time to come calling, he says, peering at me through the narrow space between door and frame.

I can't use it, I say.

What?

The suit. Can I come in?

No, he says. I'm sorry, but this is not a proper hour.

I'll be gone in the morning.

What is it you want? he asks. I hear phlegm shifting at the back of his throat.

I want to return it.

Return it?

Sell it back.

I'm sorry, he says, but that's not possible. I have no need for it. I put a good number of hours into that suit. I did exactly what you asked, and it was not easy—was not easy to keep the cost within your budget, which frankly was quite meager. So tell me, what is the problem?

I describe the glint off the gems, the arch of the ball just before it struck the woman's shin. He nods, clears his throat into a handkerchief, shuts the door. I hear the chain sliding free of its plate.

OK, he says. Come in.

The burlap curtain is drawn to one side. A fire in the small iron stove at the back of the room makes a black silhouette of the half-mannequin, casts the piles of fabric in shadow. There's a book lying open on a cot near the stove, a glass of wine within arm's reach on the floor. The only sound comes from kindling sparking in the fire.

He gestures to a child-sized chair beside the drafting table, switches on a lamp, clears away a stack of patterns.

Let me see it, he says.

I hand him the package. He unwraps it, examines the hopsacking cloth, the tiger's eye and rhinestone. The tips of his fingers are blunted, calloused—the knuckles have lost their bend. I look over the living space. The cot is padded with cushions from a discarded sofa. There's a bursting armchair, a small stack of branches by the fire, a column of books piled in a corner, a wicker hamper for his clothes.

I can discount the labor by a percentage, he says. The stitching limits the portion of material I can reuse, though there is some. As for the gems, since they are counterfeit, they are not worth much.

He lifts a store receipt off a milk crate, scribbles a column of figures on the back, circles the bottom number.

I nod.

All right, he says.

He walks into the living space, pulls the curtain shut behind him. He's left the suit on the table, folded at the waist, the torso resting on the pant legs, the arms hanging off the edges of the table. I take a last look, admiring the small bluebird he embroidered on the right shoulder, the tight black stitching that went into drawing distinct feathers on the wing and tail, the actual red and white feathers he'd pasted down to make a tuft crowning the bird's head. Maybe he'll put the suit on display—nail it to a wall or fit it for a mannequin. Most likely it will end up buried in one of his piles.

He comes back, sets the bills in my palm.

I am sorry it did not work out, he says.

I start to answer, but my voice catches, and he's already leading me to the door.

• • •

I stop in a bar that's crowded though the street outside is empty. There are tables of men playing cards, women in flounced dresses working the floor. I take a stool with my back to the room. The barman is busy clearing glasses and soaking up spilled liquor with a rag. I wave him over, order a shot and ask him to leave the bottle. The surface of the bar is pocked and peeling. The whiskey keeps me stuttering over the same calculations—number of vials divided by number of jumps, cost of the suit minus what the tailor paid plus the fine. I puncture a varnish blister with the tip of my hook, pull the coating back.

Halfway into the bottle I feel a hand on my shoulder. It's one of the women who work the floor. She's wearing a lace dress cut low. The tops of her breasts are dotted with moles, her bare arms flushed—the kind of ruddy flesh that turns white wherever you touch it. Her face is painted like a stage girl's. I pretend not to notice when she starts at my hook.

She leads me up a staircase behind the bar, into an open wooden booth, draws the curtain behind us. I lean back, shut my eyes. The booth smells of chlorine. The smell turns my head. I'm not sure if I'm standing or lying down. I feel her hands on my bare chest, her nails raking my skin.

By the time I leave, the tailor's bills are gone.

Twenty-Nine Palms, California

July 1902

You're a charlatan. You're a thief, and you won't rob the citizens of my town.

Connor wiped rain from his glasses with a handkerchief, set the handkerchief back in his blazer pocket and raised his head to the small gathering.

This man wants you to continue in your suffering, he said, so that your physical state might mirror his own sour disposition.

I'm telling you to pack up and leave.

Sir, tipsification is a vice, particularly before noon.

And yet here you are, before noon, peddling your dressed-up liquor. I know you and I know your business. You prey on people who have exhausted every legitimate avenue and have nothing more to lose.

You see, ladies and gentlemen, what this man thinks of you.

I'm the elected mayor of this town, and these are the people who elected me. You're damn right they know what I think of them. My sheriff and his men are out picking up your signs. You can fetch them at the jailhouse, which by god is where you will be if you and your fake Indian don't move on. You need a permit to hawk your wares in this town.

Sir, Connor said, I was not acquainted with the laws of your city. I would be most happy to apply—

Denied. I'll have a deputy come by to make sure you're gone. If you aren't, I doubt you'll like your accommodations.

He turned, clucked his tongue at the crowd. People padded off, glancing back now and again to see if anything more would happen. Connor started crating his medicine. I tried to help him pick the crates up into the wagon, but he waved me away.

• • •

We'd traveled an hour down the coast before he spoke again.

You agree with that highbinder, don't you? he said. You'd like to see me in jail?

I wouldn't.

You would. I see it in your posture. I hear it in your tone. You're slumming with a fraud until you can gather your nerve. Just remember, you were living like livestock when I found you.

I never—

You haven't said it because you need me. But a day is coming when you will say it. And I want you to know in advance that you're wrong. I offer a product whose efficacy has been scientifically proven—if not by chemical science, then by empirical science. For decades now, I have watched it alleviate and often relieve altogether the suffering of countless people for whom orthodox medicine had done nothing. I am not lecturing to you, I am simply telling you the truth. If I adopt the air of a charlatan, if I trick my act, as you call it, with frippery of various kinds, it's because that is what common people respond to. I debase myself for their benefit. Believe me, if my unique goal were to make money, there are better ways. I want you to take that into consideration the next time you see fit to judge me.

• • •

That night we camped in a wooded lot not far from the beach. Connor sat with his back against the bole of a pine tree, sipping from a jug of moonshine and stropping the blade of a twine-handled knife against the underside of a rawhide belt. I lay on my bedroll a few yards off, lamp raised on a rock beside me, reading the crime column from a Gazette I'd picked up in one of the towns we'd passed through.

So, Connor said, you are literate?

You thought I wasn't?

There are days I forget you can speak, he said. Perhaps I mistook you. Perhaps you're the brooding, intellectual type? Tell me, apart from local trivium, what is it you like to read?

I don't know, I said. Adventure stories.

Adventure stories? Heroines in the hands of heathens? Spaniards rescued from Turkish slave ships? That sort of thing.

I guess.

Falderal, he said. It's time you had a proper education. I'll fetch you a real adventure story.

He sheathed his knife, buckled his belt around his pants without using the loops, took up his lamp and rummaged through the wagon. He came back with a leather-bound edition, the silhouette of an ancient armada branded into the front cover.

The original, he said. And still the greatest. A book to which all other books make reference.

He handed it to me. I opened to a random page.

It's poetry, I said.

You do know something. Still, it's not poetry the way you think of poetry.

He sat again with his back to the tree.

Read it, he said.

Out loud?

Why not?

I'm tired.

Nonsense, it's early yet.

From the beginning?

Where else?

I closed the book, opened it again, turned past the title page. He stopped me before I reached the end of the first line.

I thought you said you could read?

I can.

Then you should know not to pause after each word. Do you understand the meanings?

Yes.

Then let's have a little rhythm. Begin again.

He let me go for half a page.

No, he said. That simply won't do. I understand your stumbling over foreign names, but you're butchering even the most common nouns. Have you heard of meter? Listen.

He stood, stuck out his chest like a crooner, recited the line I'd read without looking at the book.

You see, he said. Poetry is meant to be spoken, not muttered. Now get up.

I held the book in one hand and my lantern in the other. I tried to start the words deep in my chest, but I couldn't focus on the page and my voice at the same time.

Worse still, he said. You have no feel for this whatsoever. Again, from the beginning.

We kept going, back and forth, Connor swilling from his jug, calling me a dunce, a lubber, a mutt, a sot, raising his voice when I didn't flinch. My neck was slick with sweat but I wouldn't give in. Not even when day broke and Connor was still standing.

Dalkey, California

October 2, 1922

I'm lying flat on the bed, the last single-notched vial balanced on my chest. The clerk put me in the room next to Jonson's. I can hear Jonson snoring, the boy singing—something slow and sad, as though he's singing to keep his father asleep. There's a blunt throbbing at the center of my head. I close my eyes, arch my back, feel the vial roll onto my stomach. I notice the boy's gone quiet before I hear the knocking at Jonson's door.

Go on, Jonson says, get yourself some air.

I hear a woman's voice in the room, the boy's footsteps heading down the corridor. I stand, press my ear to the wall. Jonson is talking, the woman laughing. There's a pouncing on the bedsprings, a sound like a lamp faltering on the nightstand.

I catch up with the boy on the town's only commercial street, keep a full block behind. The shops are closed for the season. A month ago people were lining up to buy painted seascapes, bracelets made of oyster shells, playing cards with mermaid queens and Neptune kings. Every stool in every bar was taken, every hotel booked. Tonight, the streetlights seem lit for the boy alone.

The stores drop off, the wooden sidewalk gives way to sand. The boy slips off his shoes and socks, keeps walking towards the water. I sit on a bench and watch. The boy looks stenciled into the foreground. He rolls up his pant legs, steps to the edge of the water, holds his arms out at the sides as the current carries him backwards. The breeze off the water cuts through my coat.

The boy retreats onto the shore, takes up a clump of sea wrack and tosses it to the waves. Facing the water, he bends at the waist, lifts himself into a handstand, raises his right palm inches off the sand. He totters, then falls, tucking his chin to his chest, rounding his back and rolling through a somersault. He tries again and his legs stay raised a little longer. He's routining his act, bolstering the finish by standing on just one hand. Soon, he stops falling.

After a while, he wipes his feet clean, slips on his socks and shoes. For a moment I think I might stand, block his path, tell him what I know Jonson won't—that if he wants to see his name in lights he'll chase down that browser and not look back. But instead I lie on my side with my hook between my knees and watch through the slats until he's gone.

I take off my own shoes and socks, fold my pant cuffs. The sand cools my feet, catches in the cracked skin around my heels. I reach the area where the boy had been rehearsing. There are handprints layered one atop the other, a patch of sand rolled flat by his spine. I kneel, begin tamping down his tracks with my palm, filling in the depressions, smoothing over every disturbed surface. When I'm done, there's just a compact and trodden space.

I crouch facing the water, breathing hard, squinting into the distance, trying to separate black water from black sky. Goose pimples riffle up my spine. I pull my knees to my chest but can't stop shivering. It isn't the breeze or the ocean air. It's my body asking for what's locked in my valise.

• • •

At a little after midnight I sit with my back to the bed, hold the vial up to the light. I'm looking for what I know isn't there, a means of extracting without subtracting, a way to take what I need without weakening the vial. I roll it over on my palm, watch the silver disperse through the blue, gravitate back to the center. I pinch the vial between my thumb and forefinger, hold it straight, then on its side. I shake it gently, observe that the shards will only stray so far, that they always reverse course before touching the glass. I shake the silver with the full force of my wrist, feel the bottom stopper slip free of my thumb, watch the vial strike my knee, rebound into the air. I swipe at it with what I think is my right hand. The glass cracks, shatters against the wall. I watch the blue streaks eat into the paint, disappear into the floorboards. I crawl forward, knock away the glass with my hook, lick at the blue until my tongue turns numb.

· · ·

Jonson is waiting for me in my dressing room—a room so small we both have to stand.

You want something? I say.

Easy, he says. You ain't rich in friends.

What I salvaged of the vial is only starting to fade.

I'm guessing you want something, I say.

Listen, he says, you got two jobs, and you got to keep the one to keep the other. Truth is, you're breaking apart at both ends. There's some won't take kindly to it.

They know I've been skimming?

I know.

And you're their spy.

You figured that much. What you don't know is it ain't them you got to worry about.

What does that mean?

I told you what I can, Swain. I ain't being coy.

What about your son?

What about him?

Do they know he's working for them, too?

You can't hurt my boy, he says. I'd slit your throat if I thought you could.

It's not me who's hurting him, I say.

I'll do right by my son. You worry about yourself. I'm going to talk straight with you, Swain. No bullshit. What you're trying to hold onto is out of reach. You're done. You don't have a goddamned thing left. You know it. I'm just the one saying it. Take a trip, Swain. You've got brains. This ain't the only life for you. I'm being honest now. It would be good for you if you listened.

Tell me this, I say. Why do you care?

I done my part, Swain, he says. The next part is yours.

Oceanside, California

October 1902

I need a civilized sleep, Connor said. A civilized sleep and a little time to think.

Up and down the coast, autumn was chasing the tourists, leaving locals who'd seen us before. Nobody was buying. Nights, Connor drank and paced our camp with a pistol tucked in his pants. By morning his eyes looked as if they were leaking lamp-black.

A hotel? I said.

I'll need you to stay with the wagon.

We pulled up under the porte-cochere of a pastel-blue building with matching wood shutters on every window. A man in uniform opened the door for Connor. From where I was sitting I could see into the lobby—hand-blown chandeliers, imported plants with polished fronds, a clerk in a suit and boutonniere.

Connor returned with a key, drove the wagon onto a grass lot behind the hotel, maneuvered it between two motorized cabriolets. A stable boy came for the horse. Connor left me the rifle, carried the pistol and cash box with him.

Don't hesitate, he said. Our belongings, our future profits, are worth the life of any man who would take them. Don't hesitate.

The only light came from the moon and the hotel's windows. I watched until Connor was gone, then fired my lamp and sat for a while with my legs dangling off the back flap of the wagon, drinking from a pint of medicine. Horses whickered and pawed in the barn across the lot. I heard voices coming from the kitchen but couldn't make out their words. The air smelled of garlic and fish and something I couldn't name. When I played the Majestic, I stayed in a hotel with tessellated floors, a bath in each room, a pianist in the lobby, a fresh breakfast for every day of the week.

I spread my bedroll between crates of medicine and boxes of canned food, slid the rifle under a blanket and lay reading from a dime novel. A string band started playing somewhere inside the hotel. Vehicles kept leaving and arriving. I shut my eyes, but I wasn't tired. The medicine hadn't done anything more than coat my mouth and throat. This was the first time Connor had left me alone. Besides the cash, there was nothing anyone would know to look for. I pulled on my slicker, pocketed the bottle and blew out the lamp. I kept a row of trees between me and the hotel until I reached the street.

• • •

The theater was a converted storefront on a side road across from a small square. By the time I found it a stand-alone comic in a checkered bowler was bowing off the olio. A sketch with a plot about a cop and a woman he'd caught shoplifting took the deuce spot. For the store's façade they wheeled on a plywood cut-out that looked as if it had been painted with no drawing to work from. The applause-man laughed a beat ahead of every joke.

A local school girl danced a short routine to an off-tone piano and then a fat woman in a ragged pinafore played Mozart on a long-tooth saw. A minute into her act a small mutt ran onstage, squatted at her ankles and howled until she stopped.

The woman stomped her foot but the dog kept howling. The comic came back, shooed it away, stayed to sing three verses of an Irish ballad. A man in front yelled, The dog had it right.

The headliners followed, a pair of knock-about acrobats, bandy-legged twins who drove trick hatchets into each others skulls before somersaulting the length of the boards. They were skilled enough to improvise in mid-air, but I didn't clap. I hadn't laughed at the comic or snickered when the cop flubbed his patter. The theater's ceiling was low and its stage shallow. It had no gallery. By daylight it turned back into a store. It was a hinterland house for hinterland talent, but it was a theater with lights and wings and people who were paid to be there. Connor was wrong. I had failed. Watching wouldn't stop the chatter.

• • •

In the morning, Connor found me sitting with my back against a stack of crates, chewing a piece of pilot bread.

Put that away, he said. I've brought you a real breakfast.

He took a napkin from his jacket pocket, folded back the edges, revealed a well-cooked steak.

I thought I might carry some civilization to you, he said. Mind, we can't afford this every day of the week, but once in a great while…

Thank you, I said.

Don't mention it.

He was standing just outside the wagon, staring up at me, smiling, his skin damp with mist.

Did you sleep? I asked.

I did, he said. I did indeed. The kind of sleep that allows you to think as you rest. I have it figured out, my son. We'll be flush in no time.

We were going to leave the coast. We'd return. We weren't

giving up. But sometimes people have to be thrown upon their own resources before they will acknowledge how desperately they need saving. In the meantime, we would head inland, following a course that would have us back in California before the first snow. I wasn't going to be an Indian anymore. He had a new idea, one that would take full advantage of my enormous talent. I would be resistant at first. He wouldn't blame me if I were. But in the end I'd see it was for the best—not only for our present act, but also for my future on the stage.

Yes, he said. I know you won't be with me forever.

Salida, Colorado

October 7, 1922

I take a bus to a smaller town, then hitch a ride on a milk wagon miles out into country thick with pine. The driver lets me off at the start of a private road. I know from the mailbox that I have the right place. The road is unpaved, the ground quiet beneath a layer of brown needles. There's a fat line of smoke rising up from somewhere not too far ahead. I hear a small river or a large creek echoing out of a nearby ravine.

The road ends in a clearing that houses a cabin, a flat-bed truck, and the covered wagon that Connor and I used to travel in. The wagon's canvas top is written over in red letters, most of them faded or washed away. The cabin is slanted, square. I move behind the tree line, circle the clearing until the schooner stands between me and the cabin, then start forward. The wagon's sideboards are cracked, the bonnet torn. I take hold of the brake lever, step up on the yoke, peer inside. The clapboard shelving has been dismantled. The bed is all spider webs.

I step back onto the path, walk straight for the door. Through the mesh screen I see Connor sitting at a log table with a cup of coffee and a small cut of meat. His hair is gone on top, his flesh sags at the jowls. He's wearing a striped night shirt with an embroidered placket coming unstitched down the front.

Swain? he says, reaching for the rifle he keeps at hand.

Easy, I say. I'm not here for that.

He stands. I step inside. The walls are covered with what used to be in the wagon—a feathered tomahawk, a silver stethoscope, a shelf of antique bottles, a cardboard poster with Connor's face painted on it.

It's not like you to let someone get close, I say.

My dog died, he says. How'd you find me?

I wouldn't mind some coffee.

I want to know how?

Coffee? I ask, sitting.

I just have the one cup.

This must be a damn sight out of your way, he says, still standing. What is it you want?

Nothing you can give back.

And nothing I took away, either. He slams his open palm on the table. Remember, he says. It was you who walked out on me.

I'm not the kid I was then, I say. That won't work.

He sits, smiling. I look the cabin over. Besides the table and chairs, there's a pipe stove in the corner, a pile of worn horse blankets laid out on the floor. I spot the drawknife hanging above the back door, the teeth polished, gleaming. Connor looks with me. We're both seeing it. Water breaking over the rocks. A slice of river framed by aspen and alder. Clusters of iris on the opposite bank. But I can't see Connor, can't see myself, can't see anything beyond what I saw that night, my head turned away, my wrist tethered to a boulder with the horses' reigns, my good hand trussed to my belt. I feel insects touching down on my neck, feel the teeth tickling my wrist as Connor aligns the blade. Then nothing. In all the years of pushing my mind back the blade never breaks my skin, the oil never blisters my flesh.

So what do you want? he asks.

A gun, I say. A handgun, of course. And bullets.

You could have had a gun anywhere.

I came to you.

Why?

Curiosity.

All right, he says. Ask.

That evening in Oceanside, you knew I'd head for the theater?

I thought you might. I was watching from a window on the stairs.

I spent the rest of that night staring down a rifle.

But you're still here. If you wouldn't climb back on a wire, you weren't going to put the barrel of a gun in your mouth and pull the trigger. I said it would be good for you in the long run. Was I wrong? Your life is better because of me, not worse.

That's not for you to decide, I say.

But it's done, isn't it? We helped a lot of people, Swain. If you accepted that, your life might go a little easier.

He picks up his rifle, steps to the antique chest beside the fireplace, returns with a small nickel-plated revolver and a cardboard box. He sets the box on the table, removes the lid, flicks out the cylinder and empties the chambers one at a time into the box.

Will that do?

Does it fire?

It will once you've loaded it.

Then it'll do.

We sit for a while without talking.

Not that you're asking, he says, but I'm an inch shorter than I used to be and I can't eat more than twice a day. I've stopped dreaming at night. Lately, I've been pissing blood. I don't know a single person I knew ten years ago. Not that you're asking.

I didn't come for that either, I say.

I'm at the door when he calls me back.

If I see you again, he says, I'll know you have that.
You might want a new dog, I say.

• • •

I take up one of the last remaining vials, carve a third notch in the stopper.

I lie on the bed, eyes closed, arms at my sides, good hand wrapped around the handle of the gun. The gun feels permanent, like the prosthetic, as if my hands are now hook and barrel. I scan my body. Nothing hurts. No part of me is knotted, bruised, broken, fractured, pulled, scratched. I can't feel the mattress under my back, the pillow under my head. I raise my gun-hand toward the ceiling, cock the hammer, ease it back down.

• • •

My valises are chained in the luggage hole. We're headed for the last stop on this run. I board the bus, eye the seats, walk past Jonson and his boy and on to the back. Jonson's beside me before I've had a chance to close my eyes.

Comfy, Swain? he asks.
Too soon to tell, I say.
Why'd you do it? he asks.
Do what?
Get on this bus.
You know why.
There's time, he says. The driver ain't pulled out yet.
I'm not done.
Goddamn it, Swain, I'm trying to help you.
Don't.
He rolls his shoulders.
Take the scenery in, Swainee, he says. Don't miss a drop. This is your last ride.

Slant Rock, New Mexico

October 15, 1922

Jonson falls down drunk onstage. The boy keeps on as if his father's collapse were part of the act. Watching the boy from the wings, I think, You ought to be grateful.

That night, I sit on my valise, ear to the wall, waiting for Jonson's boy to take his nightly walk. My body aches from what I haven't put in it. Sometimes my vision blurs, sometimes what I'm looking at comes in so clear my head reels back.

Jonson is still drunk, or maybe drunk again. His words run on without any shape to them. I can feel the boy wanting to break away.

There's a knocking at Jonson's door. The boy leaves, a woman enters. I go to the window, lean my head outside, watch the boy cross the street. I feel like I might be sick, like I might vomit up not only the contents of my stomach, but the stomach itself, bringing with it intestines, esophagus, pharynx. The desert air has turned cold. I hold still at the window, let the breeze cool my skin.

I stand, pace the perimeter of the bed, bite at the inside of my cheeks to keep my teeth from quivering. The message on the call board told me to report in the morning. Jonson, no doubt, has been told to report before me.

I can hear them now, laughing, working the bedsprings.

Jonson must be feeding her liquor, or maybe something more.

There won't be time, I think. She will leave, and the boy will be back.

I take the gun from my sock, drop it in my front left pocket, step into the hall. I stand beside Jonson's door, listening. My body is breaking down, dissolving. My clothes are soaked through. One step more, I think. If not tonight, then never again.

I reach for the knob, turn it slow. I have one foot inside Jonson's room.

II

Jonson

I

From his window he could see the vacant plot where he'd buried her. A clearing in the weeds, three feet of copper pipe for a
headstone. His son was crying behind him. Jonson glanced back,
spotted thin lines of blood breaking through the hives.

You're going to leave scars, he said.

He took a small pair of scissors from the window sill and
knelt beside the basket.

Easy now, he said.

Straightening the boy's fingers one at a time, he trimmed
the nails halfway down.

He lifted his son from the basket and laid him atop a faded
blanket in the claw-foot tub that took up most of the apartment's only room. The crying bounced around the basin, spiked
abruptly upward. Jonson reached for the bottle and rag he kept
beneath the tub. He soaked a swatch of cloth in brandy, wrapped
the fabric around his finger, coated the boy's gums. He drank
some himself, then reached the fingers of his free hand into a
small container of foundation left over from his stage career. He
rubbed the tan make-up evenly over his son's hives, caked it over
the cuts and scabs. The boy fussed, slapped at his father's hand,
kicked at the blanket where it caught his feet.

All right, now, Jonson said.

He leaned back, surveying his work. The welts were covered over, but the boy's face appeared sunburned, almost brown. Jonson loosened the drawstring on the final sack of his wife's effects, those he had not been able to sell, rummaged through until he uncovered a small jar of white powder. He dusted the boy's cheeks, lightened the skin by a full shade.

That'll do, he said, returning his son to the basket, packing a day bag for himself.

A succession of trolleys carried them through narrow streets lined with jerrybuilt row houses, then outsized boulevards dotted with bistros and boutiques. An old woman paused over the basket to smile and coo. Johnson turned away, squinted out at the street, tried to still the bobbing derbies with his eyes.

The final trolley let them off just shy of Ray's building. A doorman with tassled epaulettes called upstairs, then let him pass. Jonson rode the elevator to the penthouse, rang a small ivory pushbutton, trailed a uniformed maid into a parlor done up in damask wallpaper and walnut wainscoting. She gestured to a leather Morris chair, pulled the door shut behind her.

Friendly, Jonson said.

He set his son on the floor, toured the room. There was a marble fireplace with steel doors and brass andirons, a collection of silver-plated samovars on the mantle above. A small oak desk housed a hooded typewriter with no ribbon or paper. It was a good while before Ray entered.

Tell that lady who let me in she needs to dust the insides, Jonson said, balancing a small samovar on his palm.

Please sit, Ray said.

We have something to talk about?

Sit.

They sat in matching loveseats, Jonson's son asleep between them, his basket filling the marble coffee table. Ray leaned forward, seemed to be counting the hives through the foundation.

That's just shit babies get, Jonson said.

I'm not in the market.

A loan, then, Jonson said. I already got people interested in my services.

What people?

A liner out of New York. Room and board plus cash in my sock drawer.

How much are you asking?

I got that doctor after me.

How much?

A grand.

Is that all?

You being sarcastic? My wife's dead.

You'd never pay me back.

I could say I would.

I know somebody who might be interested, Ray said. In the boy.

He took a pad and pencil from his jacket pocket, wrote out a name and address, tore the sheet free. He offered it to Jonson, then pulled it back, set it on the table beside the basket.

Are you sure this is what she would want? he asked. For you to pawn her child?

Hers? I thought he was at least part mine, Jonson said. Maybe you know something I don't.

Don't be an ass.

Maybe he's yours all along?

If you want something, you're going about it the wrong way.

I want back onstage. Get me on a circuit and I'll keep him.

I can't.

Why?

You're not solo talent.

Jonson plucked at the stitching of the arm rests with his fingernails and stared across the table. Ray was tallow-faced, sloe-eyed. Creases cut through his forehead like runnels. Jonson hesitated, then took up the sheet of paper.

I hope you ain't waiting on a commission, he said.

• • •

He walked the thirty blocks to save on fare. The streets, empty at first, began to fill with vendors and school kids, then stock brokers, realtors, lawyers—bloated men in tailored suits who didn't know what to make of him or the baby he was carrying. He set his son down at the center of a busy sidewalk, straddled the basket and shook out his wrists. People parted around him, seemed to quicken their pace.

The skyscrapers gave way to row houses; the sidewalks began again to empty. The air was cold for late October but his undershirt clung to the small of his back and his forehead was damp. He set the basket on the concrete stoop, wiped sleep from his son's eyes, stood studying the boy's new home. The windows, set close together, appeared just wide enough to fit a child's torso; the beige bricks were packed in around slight lines of mortar.

He rang the bell, waited. An undersized boy of five or maybe six let him in, then turned and ran up the stairs. Jonson followed. Already he could hear a piano poorly played, a host of young voices blotting one another out. The woman Ray had mentioned stood sideways in a doorway off the third-floor landing.

Mr. Jonson? she said. Ray sent word you'd be coming. I'm sorry to hear about your wife.

She spoke like a singer. Like a woman who'd swallowed a lot of air.

Thank you, ma'am, he said.

Inside, there were children clinging to battered sofas and

chairs, sitting cross legged on rugs, pressing against walls. Some were dressed in costumes, others in their bed clothes. A girl in pigtails failed at handstand after handstand; two small boys helped a kid in his teens balance himself atop a unicycle. There were pancakes grilling in the adjoining kitchenette, dirty dishes stacked on a straw mat in the far corner. The woman clapped her hands, scattered the children to a back room.

Leona, she said to the girl at the piano, keep an eye on those hot cakes. To Jonson she said, This is no place for a kid to get lonely.

I can see that.

Now, where's your boy?

Right here.

She glanced at the basket.

Him?

Yes ma'am.

Oh son, she said. Ray should've known better. Managers pay by the head. That ain't a head yet.

He comes from show stock.

Bring him back in four or five years. I need kids who can sing, dance. At least talk and walk. Ray should've known better.

Yes ma'am, he should have, Jonson said.

Outside, he set the basket atop a garbage can, spit on his thumb and wiped the boy's cheeks clean.

Go on, he said. You can fuss all you want now.

He stopped at a diner across from the doctor's office, the restaurant where he'd eaten with Ginny after each of her visits. It was patronized by staff from the nearby hospital, decorated with finger paintings from the children's ward. The waitresses' uniforms looked to be made from the same material as a surgeon's mask. Ginny would order breakfast food, even in the late afternoon—eggs sunny-side up, toast burnt. She'd break the yolks with the desiccated bread, leave the whites on her plate.

Jonson took a seat by the window, ordered coffee and asked for a pen. He quieted his son with a sugar cube, sat watching the passersby, wondering how many of them would have done better than he had done, if there were some key he'd missed, something that appeared obvious to everyone but him.

He opened his napkin on the table, started to write.

> Doctor—
> Its done for me in this world.
> Keep him safe.
> X

He left money pinned under his empty coffee cup, walked as far as the door, then returned to the table and took back the tip. He stuffed the change in his sock, started across the street with his son.

The doctor would be at the hospital all morning, interviewing patients, waking them to ask how they'd slept, pressing on their injured parts to make sure it hurt in all the right places. Jonson entered the lobby, set the basket against the office door, draped the napkin, writing-side up, over the handle. He crouched down, laid an open hand across the boy's stomach.

Sorry, he said. It just ain't in me.

He started for the train station with his wrist throbbing from the absent weight. He'd be in New York by next morning, would be sailing for Europe in two days time. He walked a half-dozen blocks, sat on the curb, told himself he had nothing to regret: he'd done what he could, hurt nobody. He tried and failed to push his mind forward.

He stood, headed back.

II

The baby was laughing, slapping his hands together as though applauding whatever he'd found funny. Jonson transferred him from basket to basin, took a shoebox from under the tub, removed a razor blade, a small jar of peach puree, a tube of soporifics left over from the early stages of Ginny's illness. The pills were dwindling: a week at most and they would be gone. He slid one out, set a spoonful of puree on the floor, held the pill between thumb and forefinger and scraped at its edge with the razor blade until a fine blue dust coated the puree. He returned the remainder of the pill to the tube, stirred the puree with the tip of his little finger, then offered the spoon to his son. Once the boy was asleep, Jonson dug what money he had out of his socks, set aside a ten-dollar bill and spread the rest between his back pockets. He shut the light, locked the door behind him.

The pool hall was empty save for two men playing at a far table—brothers, their features near identical, separated by a half-dozen years or more. There were stickered valises and a damaged guitar case propped against the wall behind them; their clothes were crumpled, their shirttails untucked, their hair uncombed. The older wore a fedora hat with a string running brim to brim beneath his chin; the younger wore glasses made of two different colored frames soldered together at the nose. The older amused himself with trick shots he couldn't execute, made fake bets, blamed the younger for every miss. The younger powdered his cue, took careful aim.

Jonson wracked up an adjacent table. He broke, put a striped ball in a side pocket, banked three more, then cursed as he missed a straight-on shot. The brothers applauded.

A good run, the older said.

I'm out of practice, Jonson said. Wouldn't mind someone to spar with.

A wager? the older said.

With you?

Oh no, not me, the older said. He took off his hat, stuck it on his brother's head.

All right, Jonson said, setting a ten on the felt.

We can cover that, the older said.

The younger wracked up the balls, returned the hat to his brother.

He don't say much, Jonson observed.

Can't talk, the older said. He can hear, though. Perfect pitch. Can pick a tune out of the air and play it on your instrument of choice.

And what do you do? Jonson asked.

Me? I'm the laughs.

He pulled a rust-colored flask from his back pocket.

Want some?

Only if he does.

The mute smiled, took a sip and passed the flask to Jonson. Jonson tilted his head back, tasted something like kerosene cut with uncooked grains of rice.

Home brew, the older said.

Whose home?

Jonson stepped to the table, pocketed a string of shots before his turn was up.

You know, he said, moving aside, a third head might bump you up in the order.

You looking to get back in?

Might be.

What are you offering?

Song, dance, a little piano, he said. And I can deliver a line as good as anyone.

We don't have a lot of dialogue just now.

I could add that dimension.

True. It would have to be worth paying for.

The mute banked the eight ball; Jonson placed a second ten on the table.

Funny our paths never crossed before, the older said.

Half my act died, Jonson said. Took her a good long time.

The older drained the flask, slipped a second from his pocket, broke it in before passing it to Jonson. Jonson hesitated, felt his eyes strain to keep the balls in focus. He looked across the table, trying to determine if the mute was immune, or if the liquor was working on him, too. He took a sip, passed it on.

Your turn, the older brother said.

Jonson rushed his shot as though trying to outpace the alcohol. The mute stepped up, finished the game.

All I got now is some ones, Jonson said.

When the flask came back around, Jonson weighed it in his palm, found it no lighter than the last time he'd drank from it. A shard of pain cut through his chest. He wrapped his lips around the mouth, blocked the liquor with his tongue. Smiling, he passed the flask to the older brother, then picked up a cue stick and stove it across his head. The older stumbled, turned, came at Jonson. Jonson kicked out his knee, brought the splintered wood sideways down his face. The mute backed up; the attendant stepped out from behind his desk, club in hand.

You got some hustlers here, Jonson said.

That right?

Tell him, mute, Jonson said.

The mute said nothing.

Oh, bullshit, Jonson said.

He leaned down, grabbed the older by the hair, held the jagged end of the stick to his throat.

Cash on the table.

The attendant edged forward.

You're good where you are, Jonson said.

The mute pulled a fistful of crumpled bills from his pocket, began counting.

I want what I would have won, Jonson said, raising the stick.

All right, the mute said. All right.

You see, Jonson told the attendant.

He bent down, pocketed the flask on his way out.

• • •

Five cents got him in for what was left of the shows, two cents more got him a bag of roasted peanuts. He sat alone in his row, savoring each nut, taking slow sips from the older brothers' flask. He stared ahead, unaware of what was happening onstage—only that there was color, movement, sound—then a spate of stillness, quiet—then color, movement, sound again. He tongued the mouth of the flask, fingered the corners of the bag in search of a last nut.

He stopped at a liquor store, emptied a fresh pint of whiskey before returning to his son.

• • •

The window had fallen shut while he slept; the room smelled of vomit, shit, alcohol. Someone was shaking him. Jonson rolled onto his back, saw the old woman who managed the place standing over him, felt her bare foot on his chest, felt his temples pulsing in time to the baby's screams.

Out, she said. Out, out, out.

What?

Too many complaints.

Now?

Now.

Let me get dressed, he said. Change my son.

I'll be in the hall.

Jonson stood, looked the room over, realized that he had never bothered to look it over before. For him, it had been parts with no sum: a tub, a window, a wall bifurcated by a steel pipe. If he sat in the tub facing in one direction, he saw the door but not the window; if he sat facing the other direction, he saw the window but not the door. If he stood looking outside, he had no sense that he was standing with his back to a room that contained a tub, a door, a steel pipe.

Come on now, the landlady called.

A minute, Jonson said.

He opened the window, relieved himself into the alley below.

III

All right, Ray said. All right. I think I've got something to keep you afloat.

Room and board?

You should be able to work it out with her.

Her?

Ray wrote a name and address on a slip of paper.

A Madame?

With the business I throw her way, she can't afford not to take you on.

There must be acts on the circuit that feel the same, Jonson said. I don't have to go it alone.

I couldn't, Ray said.

You could.

I won't. I have a reputation. I promised Ginny I'd look out for you, but by God...

Jonson held up a hand.

Best stop there, he said.

• • •

The walk up the macadamized driveway took him past flower beds, sculpture gardens, Rolls Royces. The portico was large enough for a man to live in, its roof doubling as a lanai with marble balustrade and matching chaise longue. The Madame came to the door in a blue silk gown and diamond earrings, a fresh-picked corsage pinned to her breast. She'd rouged over the liver spots on her neck, wore opera-length gloves to cover the backs of her hands.

Ray sent me, Jonson said.

Right, she said, eyeing the basket.

Inside, there were women with their legs crossed running the length of a batik-print sofa, one per cushion. A dark-skinned woman in a sarong. A pale blonde with her hair bobbed and marcelled. An Asian girl in a jewel-studded bra and grass skirt.

He's here for me, the Madame said.

They quit smiling, let their shoulders go slack as they stood and disbanded, looking more like girls in costumes than women competing for a fare.

This way, she said.

She led him through a set of stained-glass doors into an adjoining room—a bar, newly constructed, dust still settling on the oak floor, a mammoth man in overalls and shirt sleeves coating the stools with shellac. Jonson and the Madame sat on opposite sides of a small, light-grained table. The Madame drank from a glass of clear, straight liquid, offered him nothing.

What's wrong with your kid? she asked.

Ever have any of your own?

Never wanted any.

She glared into the basket as though forcing herself to stare down something repugnant.

They get bumps on their skin. Nothing to it.

All right, she said, pointing to a piano in the far corner. Let's hear you.

He played a song he'd sung with his wife, a happy little ballad, one of the few songs he knew by heart. He sang both parts, hitting the keys soft, covering his playing with his voice.

That'll do, she said. Just keep it up tempo. The bar is an add-on. It opens in three days. I want to hear you practicing until then. Pay is eight dollars a month plus room and board for you and your kid. Room is in the basement—I can't have a baby crying upstairs. One of the girls will show you around. Your job is simple: play when I tell you to play, stop when I tell you to stop. Max will handle any fights, but this isn't that kind of place. In the meantime, I'll get a doctor to look at your kid.

Obliged, Jonson said.

She motioned for him to wait in the lobby. He sat where the whore in the sarong had sat, let his body drop into the cushions. He felt as if his limbs had been struggling to keep pace with one another and now for the first time in a long while they could rest in unison. He shut his eyes, heard his son breathing in his sleep.

The girl assigned to show him around smiled, bowed her head, called herself Cynthia. She was young with a young voice, pretty beneath the paint.

What do you think so far? she asked.

This could work, Jonson said. Better than a boat.

I'll show you where you'll stay.

The basement was well ordered, but crowded. A central aisle cut through long side aisles of identical and carefully stacked cardboard boxes. The concrete floor was swept clean, the ceiling dusted for cobwebs. Halfway down the center aisle was a cot set atop an area rug, a floor lamp plugged into an extension chord, a small bookcase for him to fill, an H&M trunk for his belongings. There were mouse traps at the mouth of every side aisle, most of them empty.

Not bad, Jonson said. You fix this up yourself?

You can make any place nice, she said.

I don't see anywhere for a baby sleep.

I didn't know there was one. I can get a crib. And a blanket. Light blue. Or dark blue, if you like.

Either'll work, Jonson said.

OK, she said. I'll let you get settled.

Jonson waited for her to leave, but she stood there, running her palms over the pleats of her skirt, glancing about as though she'd misplaced something in mid-air.

I'll be all right now, Jonson said.

The sound of his voice seemed to startle her.

. . .

He played from early morning to late evening, plucking out the few songs he remembered, filling in the lyrics he'd forgotten. Cynthia sat with his son in the garden out back; on breaks, he'd walk to the window, watch. She'd laid out a blanket on the grass, was encouraging the baby to crawl.

While Jonson played, Max worked on the bar—sanding, polishing, stocking. He was slow moving, hadn't once spoken to Jonson, didn't seem to notice the piano.

Now and again Jonson heard a gathering in the parlor. Now and again the Madame checked in, set her glass on the piano, asked why he always seemed to be playing the same song.

It's been a while, he said.

Can you read music?

Better than words.

I don't doubt it.

That night, Cynthia was waiting with his boy in the basement, sitting rigid on the edge of the cot, reading from a thick book. She looked, Jonson thought, as though she felt someone had been watching her for a long while. She was pretty in a way that had nothing to do with sex, in a way that would dissolve as soon as she tried to be pretty. Jonson cleared his throat.

The doctor came to see him, she said. He left an ointment to put on, morning and evening.

Jonson bent over the basket. The boy's skin was oily, his tufts of hair washed and combed.

He's going to be fine, she said.

That the Bible? Jonson asked, nodding at the book on her lap.

No, she said. Just a novel.

I'm sorry to hear about your wife, she said.

It took her a damn long time.

She remained perched on the cot, stiff-backed, hands folded on her lap, looking as though she wanted to speak but was awaiting permission.

What's your novel about? he asked.

She smiled, seemed surprised.

A foundling, she said. Left on the doorstep of a wealthy family. The family decides to keep her. Her sisters and brother are jealous because their father dotes on her and she's bright and pretty. When the father dies, she's sent away to a boarding school where she does well in her classes but can't get on with the headmaster. That's as far as I've gotten.

A hard luck case, Jonson said. Don't worry, she'll be fine.

You think so?

No one would ruin their eyes over a shit life that stayed shit.

No, she said. I guess they wouldn't.

Now get, Jonson said. I'm tired.

Lying on his cot with the lights out, he pictured himself as headmaster, Cynthia as his charge. But the image remained static, the figures unable to move their arms or legs, so that after a while he gave up and sat in the dark with his eyes open.

IV

He played for three days while Max readied the bar. The Madame brought him sheet music, a large stack, enough to fill a six-hour shift. Max worked steadily, starting, stopping, taking his breaks at the same time every day, as if he'd parceled out the work in advance, as if he knew how many strokes and brushstrokes it would take to sand and polish the bar. He never spoke, though on the third morning he nodded, and Jonson nodded back.

The Madame made regular rounds. Sometimes she would sit with him on the bench, sing along, applaud at the song's end. Other times she would curse Ray, bellow at Max, scream until her voice was gone. Once, she placed a vase of daisies on the piano, stopped to touch their petals, continued on, spoke to Max, turned, crossed the room, shattered the vase on her way out.

Now and again she made her tour in the company of a silver-haired man with padded shoulders and a long zoot chain. They walked arm in arm, her manner deferential—a saleswoman accentuating strengths, glossing flaws. She never introduced him, though he made a point of smiling at Max, at Jonson, at the girls.

Cynthia would be waiting for him in the early morning, the baby asleep, a new novel open on her lap. The crib had arrived, the shelves were stacked with books and sheet music.

He standing in the way of your work? Jonson asked.

I get in my hours, she said.

Well, then, Jonson said, I won't keep you.

I've got a surprise, she said.

Surprise?

She disappeared down a nearby aisle, came back wheeling a rack of men's clothes.

Mine? he said.

Yours, she said.

He toured the rack, rubbing swatches of fabric between his fingers, holding up ties to shirts, shirts to jackets. There was a midnight-blue tuxedo with a rolled collar faced in silk, a single-breasted black suit with matching cumberbund and bow tie, a patterned waistcoat, a gray smoking jacket with satin lining. Balanced on the base of the rack were a pair of two-toned English Brogues.

You pick all this out? Jonson asked.

I did. The Madame trusts me with her money.

You did fine, Jonson said. Real fine.

Aren't you going to try something on?

Not with you standing here.

I'll turn my back.

I'm a modest man, Jonson said. I'm guessing you don't know many of those.

The shoes were tight at the shanks, wide at the toe. He stripped to the waist, slid on the smoking jacket. There was a full-length mirror affixed to one end of the rack. Jonson stood before it, tapped out some slow scuffs and chugs, couldn't tell if his limbs had stiffened or were fighting the newly starched clothes. He watched himself, compared what he saw to what he believed his wife had seen, felt she'd been gone for far longer than one short summer.

He walked the length of the main aisle, the shoes giving a little at the toes, came to a room the size of a small tool shed. Switching on the light, he found a sink, a workbench, coffee cans full of nails, bolts, screws, hammers of different sizes, saws hanging in no particular order, a stack of old newspapers, a small window looking up into the underside of a bush. On the floor he discovered an open box of unmarked pint bottles. He picked one up, popped the cork, smelled something stronger than the older brother's home brew. Screwing the cork back down, he slipped the bottle into his jacket pocket.

He lay on his cot, flipping through a picture book while he drank. The pictures told the story of a stork who'd lost the baby he was supposed to deliver. The bird had injured its wing, was forced now to retrace his steps by land and sea. The book showed the stork on the deck of a ship, in the cab of a truck, in the cockpit of a plane. The people involved looked sympathetic as they shook their heads no.

Cynthia came back for the baby at eight, dressed in a paisley skirt with a small train, a canvas bag hanging from one shoulder. Jonson kept his eyes shut, his breathing heavy. Lying with a pillow over his head, a sheet pulled up to his neck, he drifted off again, dreamt of nothing in particular—flashes of color, images with no story.

• • •

The finished bar looked like it belonged to a hotel few people could afford. Everything matched: the tables were evenly spaced, the candles placed squarely at the center—the chairs, table tops, floor, bar all glazed the same deep mahogany. Stained glass windows hung inches from the walls, electric lamps lighting them from behind. The wine rack was made of solid brass, the bottles arranged by shade from white to red. The girls who worked the room looked more like bridesmaids than whores.

The Madame made a final inspection, measuring the spaces between the tables, holding her palm over lit candles, taking each girl by the chin, eyeing her make-up, adjusting her wig.

The clientele began to show. The girls dispersed—two for the bar, two for the floor. They flirted before they'd touch, held out for a second round before they'd agree to anything. When one girl left, another entered. The money was flowing upstairs and down.

Max was free and easy behind the bar, his collar unbuttoned, his sleeves rolled up. He knew when to laugh, when to lean in. He reached for the right bottle every time.

The stained glass faded behind smoke; the voices grew louder than Jonson's playing. He was decoration, one more thing the patrons could believe they were paying for. It made the keys feel lighter, as though the piano were playing itself, as though he weren't there at all.

V

His two-toned shoes were broken in. His son could stand, even stumble. He'd talked to Max, learned he was the Madame's nephew, that he had a boy he'd never met.

Cynthia gave him nightly reports.

He's a smart baby, she said.

You can tell?

He pays attention, she said.

To what?

Birds, squirrels, my finger when I point up and down. Songs, mostly. He has favorites. He has ones he doesn't like.

You sing to him?

All the time.

Let's hear.

I'm not any good, she said.

You're good enough for my son.

He's a baby.

A smart baby.

I'm shy.

How shy could you be?

All right, she said. I'll sing his favorite. But I've got to sing it to him.

So be it.

She lifted the baby from his crib. He fussed, rubbed his eyes, settled on her lap. She gave him her finger to teeth on, cleared her throat. The boy smiled and slapped at her necklace. She sang louder, skirling off key. Jonson made mental corrections, lowering her register, relaxing her spine, watching her morph into Ginny, then reemerge abruptly in her own form.

So, what do you think? she asked.

I think you're abusing my kid.

Oh, she said.

She stood, chittering in place, then lay the baby in his crib. She gathered her belongings, started for the stairs.

I didn't mean it, Jonson called. You sing fine.

She kept on, hugging her bag, her strides uneven, her shoulders banging columns of crates.

Shit and hell, he said.

He sat for a while, then walked into the side room, dug out a fresh pint, carried it back to his living space. Canting against a support beam, he drank, staring down into the crib, searching the boy's features for any sign of his mother, finding only mottled skin, tufts of hair, pads of flesh.

You're what she left me, he said. But I wish it was different.

•   •   •

The man was touching a lot for what he'd bought. Max would have let it go, but this was a girl he looked after more than the others. She was just under five feet, small boned even for her height, younger than Cynthia. Max watched the man take her hands, first one, then the other, and slide them beneath his cutaway coat. The man was fat: the girl could not reach her arms even part way around his waist without her breasts meeting his stomach, without his legs straddling her body. The girl smiled, eased her hands back, slapped the man's chest. She started to move away, but he took hold of her forearms. Max said something. The man lifted a stack of bills from his shirt pocket, peeled off the top few, secured them beneath his glass. Max stepped from behind the bar.

It was the man who swung first. Max side-stepped, grabbed the man's ear, forced his head against the bar. Jonson stopped playing. Max was leaning in close, talking low. The whore was pleading. A table's worth of men rose. Jonson crossed the room, sidled in front of them, stood with his back to Max.

I'll make this right, he said.

He turned, took Max's wrist, twisted until the ear came free.

That's good, Jonson said. He knows now.

Max knocked him away; the man's friends advanced. Jonson reached across the bar, grabbed the serrated knife Max used to cut lemons.

You got two choices, he said. You can drink and fuck on the house all night, or someone can get his throat cut.

Your man was out of line.

And it'll cost him, Jonson said. Right now, I'm making you an offer.

OK, the tallest one said. All right.

That all right with you, Max?

Swell, Max said.

Jonson waited for the small crowd to disperse, then started back, spotted the Madame watching from the doorway. She nodded toward a table in the far corner. He turned, saw the silver-haired man with padded shoulders raise his glass.

The Madame appeared again at close, a bottle of clear liquid in one gloved hand, a full glass in the other.

What do you drink? she asked Jonson.

Most anything.

By preference?

Whiskey.

Max, she called. A bottle of whiskey and a glass. You can straighten in the morning.

They sat at a corner of the bar, Jonson with his bottle, the Madame with hers.

Tell me something about yourself, she said. Her speech wasn't slurred, but the vowels were long, the volume turned high.

I don't want to bore you.

And I don't want to be bored. Start with your wife.

She's dead.

That much I know. How?

An inch at a time.

Cancer?

Not that anyone could name.

Doctors are gods or they're useless.

They charge either way.

Was she a looker?

Not at the end.

No one is, she said. Jonson watched her in the mirror behind the bar. Light pooled in the foundation beneath her eyes. This time of night, everything about her appeared rucked and water-buckled. She had been young, Jonson thought, but never beautiful.

You talk like you live, she said. Not a jot more than what's needed. I'll tell you what I think I know. Your wife was all the people you had, and you were it for her. She was the talent, you were the man of qualities. You made her feel safe. You know how to handle yourself, and you don't mind playing the supporting role. That's a rare combination in a man. You loved her, or else you feel you owe her. I know because you haven't fucked one of my girls yet.

I thought they were off limits.

She sniggered.

You can't legislate fucking, she said. If you could, I wouldn't be in business.

I guess you wouldn't.

All right, she said. Your turn. What about me?

I couldn't tell you.

I think you could. We have things in common.

Like?

You're a widower and I'm a widow. Neither of us has the stomach for what most people would call real work.

True, Jonson said.

But I've been where you are and even then I didn't hesitate. I didn't stall. I wouldn't know how to.

Is that what I'm doing?

She must have been one hell of a woman.

Jonson nodded.

But either way, he said, I never wanted much.

An invaluable trait in a man of qualities.

• • •

His son woke him for the first time in a long while; Jonson sat, drew the cot close to the crib, started the crib rocking. He patted the boy's backside, found it dry.

He lay back down, shut his eyes but couldn't sleep. Switching on the light, he pulled his wife's photo, the only photo he'd kept, from between two books. It showed her in profile, standing on the porch of a newly restored farmhouse. She had a dancer's body, lean, with a young girl's flesh still padding her face. The picture had been taken on the last day of their country vacation. There had been corn out front and out back, near ripe, the stench of fertilizer floating in from a larger farm to the south.

We're trying on a new life, Ginny said.

It smells like cow patty.

They sat on a swing on the wrap around porch, watching the sun decline, Jonson with his feet on the railing, Ginny lying with her head on his lap, wearing the striped shirt he sometimes wore onstage.

Look at that, Jonson said, letting his feet drop.

What?

Hawk, he said.

Where?

Right there.

Where?

Right in front of us, he said. Coasting with its wings out.

She stood, shielded her eyes.

Beautiful, she said.

You can't see it. I know you can't.

• • •

I need you to tend bar, the Madame said.

Max been fired?

He's coming with me. We'll be gone overnight.

All right, Jonson said. I can pour liquor as good as anybody.

I've marked the bottles, she said, so keep the money right. The girls will look after themselves.

Yes ma'am. Going anywhere in particular?

Family visit.

If I need to reach you?

You won't.

Jonson looked at her. It was as if she wanted him to know that she was lying, that there was no family trip. She was peeking his curiosity, planting a seed.

When do I start?

Now.

Jonson spoke little, drank what the patrons left behind. He studied them without pretending not to. They had money; they wore ascot ties, handspun lisle socks. An octogenarian wrapped in a carmine scarf sat sipping from a kir, trembling slightly. A fiddlebacked father counseled his obese son over a carafe of lemon vodka. Jonson imagined Cynthia beneath their bloated hands, their flab, their breath.

It was late when he closed. He cracked a window against the smoke, locked the French doors from the inside, sat with a near-empty bottle of calvados and another of scotch. He dropped the cadavers in the bin, uncapped a fresh gallon of bourbon, drank it a quarter down while he polished the zinc and mopped the floor. The mix of liquors turned the sconce lights candent, sent the pulse of his footsteps caroming up his spine.

Downstairs, he found Cynthia lying on his cot, reading. She sat up, swung her feet to the floor.

I've been thinking, she said, looking over at the crib. You could take my room. I wouldn't mind it down here.

He been complaining about me? Jonson said, sitting beside her.

Of course not.

Listen, Jonson said. Why you?

What?

Why you? You're pretty enough.

I don't understand.

Why'd she stick you with the baby? You buck in bed?

No.

Did something happen? The money must be better upstairs. Don't you like fucking?

It's not that.

Show me.

Show you what?

Show me you like fucking.

I can't.

Why not?

I can't.

She was standing, open-mouthed, rubbing her hands over her arms, tamping down goose flesh. Jonson moved toward her. She stutter-stepped through a half-circle, began to run.

All right, then, Jonson called, dropping sideways onto the cot.

He pulled the lamp's plug, lay scrolling through the Madame's girls, able to conjure their names but not their faces, their costumes but not their bodies.

VI

The Madame returned as the bar was opening, asked Jonson for a glass of ice and a bottle of gin.

Ice?

A special occasion.

So the trip was good?

No small talk.

All right.

It was a great fucking trip. Every bit of it. How'd we do here?

Fine.

Let me see.

He reached under the bar and pulled out a lidless shoebox packed with rolls of cash, one roll per denomination.

Looks about right.

That all?

I'm too damn happy to count.

She slid the box toward her, took out a thick roll of ones, handed it to Jonson.

A down payment on your loyalty.

I won't say no.

Of course you won't.

Max came in, looking frayed, beat down, his belt running

outside the loops, scratches on his neck showing through a full day's growth.

What happened to you? Jonson asked.

Nothing.

Looks like something.

I said it's nothing.

He plays too rough with my nephews, the Madame said. He forgets he's not a child, that somewhere in the world he has a son of his own.

That ain't right, Max said.

To Jonson he said, Get out from behind my bar.

Sit and have a drink with us, the Madame said.

It's almost time to open.

I say when it's time to open. Now drink.

I ain't thirsty.

You're not anything. Sit your ass down and drink.

To Jonson she said, Whiskey. In a pint glass.

No, Max said, standing.

Do you always have to spoil every goddamned thing? she said. Sit or get the fuck out and don't come back.

Jonson set a glass on the bar; the Madame pulled a capsule from her brazier, split it open and emptied the contents into the whiskey.

Drink, she told Max again. I need you relaxed. And quiet.

I am relaxed.

Bullshit. I won't listen to any more of your goddamn whining.

OK, he said. You're right.

Show me.

She stood, lifted the glass. Max clasped his hands behind his back and opened his mouth.

That's right, she said, resting the lip of the glass against his teeth, tilting it up.

Jonson, she said. You've got the bar one more night.

. . .

He was up and dressed when Cynthia came for his son.

I'm sorry, he said. For what I remember.

It's all right.

You like eggs?

Sometimes.

This one of those times?

It could be.

He led her to the kitchen, sat her at the head of a narrow table and lowered his son into a high chair. The day's milk was standing at the back door. Jonson searched the cabinets, the ice box, toured the scullery, gathering an assortment of fruit, a hunk of marbled cheese, a half dozen eggs, a sack of pearl onions, a wire basket filled with green and red peppers. He peeled a kiwi, a banana, a tangerine, broke them up and arranged them in a ceramic bowl.

Finger food, he said.

You know your way around a kitchen.

I had practice.

The omelets filled their plates, browned peppers and onions jutting up through patches of singed egg white. Cynthia cut bits from the edges, fed them to Jonson's son.

You're going to give him gas.

He likes it, she said. Better than cereal.

She took a bite herself. The boy grabbed at her sleeve, tugged her arm back.

See?

Don't let him bully you.

This is nice, Cynthia said. You did this for your wife?

It's just breakfast.

It's nice.

He sat looking at her, trying to forget the thing he knew about her. She was just a woman, a little older than a girl, eating breakfast, wearing a modest autumn dress, a full-moon locket dangling from a lanyard around her neck.

What's inside? Jonson asked, pointing.

The locket?

She slid the lanyard over her head, set the locket on the table and sprung the lid, revealing an intaglio print of an old woman in profile.

Who's this? Jonson asked.

I think she's my grandmother.

You think?

I've had it since my mother died. Since before I can remember.

Jonson set the locket on his palm and lifted it closer. The woman appeared bone-dry and unblinking, a fossil baked in a desert landscape.

I talk to her sometimes, Cynthia said. Or else she talks to me. She gives me advice. Comforts me. She tells me the world is different than it seems.

She looks like the type to know, Jonson said.

Cynthia lifted a cloth napkin, wiped food from around the baby's mouth.

He won't have that problem, she said.

What problem?

He'll have you to talk to, she said. He won't need to make anyone up.

Sometimes fake people are better, Jonson said.

She studied her plate as though searching out a wayward crumb.

That sounds smart, she said. But it isn't.

Jonson smiled.

I guess you owe me.

Men make me up, she said. They call me by different names. Women they knew or wish they knew. They tell me how to act. Not all of them, but some.

Jonson began clearing the table, collecting fruit rinds, wiping rings from beneath their cups.

Why do you think they do that? she asked.

He stood over her.

You mean would I do that?

She hesitated, then nodded.

Cause of my wife?

She nodded again. Jonson couldn't decide if she meant to rile him, or if there was something she really wanted to know.

I tried, he said. And I failed. I guess I don't have the imagination.

She rose to help him with the dishes.

That's good, she said.

• • •

The only patrons had moved upstairs; Max was leaning across the bar, talking to one of the girls, stroking her shoulder. Jonson and the Madame took a small table in the far corner.

I wish he would exercise something like discretion, she said, eyeing her nephew. I wouldn't care if it was insincere.

You worry about him?

There's no bottom too deep for him to find.

But you keep him around.

He serves his purpose.

What about Cynthia?

What about her?

You worry about her?

That girl is brilliant. If she were a man, or if she had people...

You have money. You could be her people.

The Madame smiled.

Maybe Max isn't the only one I have to watch for.

It ain't that.

What then?

I think you know. That's why you've got her watching my kid.

You mean she isn't built for this?

Something like that.

When I found Cynthia she was cowering in an alley, wearing a kitchen apron and nothing else. Bleeding from I won't say where. She didn't know what had happened. She couldn't remember her name. I'd say I am her people.

You found her, or someone brought her to you?

Is there a difference? She's smart. I know for a fact there are clients who pay her just to talk.

She remind you of you at your age?

No. For me everything was simple. I liked fucking better than sewing.

Sure, but fucking only got you so far.

You haven't known her as long as I have. She's progressing.

Jonson grinned.

You kind of collect people, don't you? he said.

I cultivate loyalty.

You're sentimental.

I believe in second chances. I'll admit to feeling some attachment. I can reconcile that with business by promising myself I'll never offer a third chance. It isn't that I'm hard, it's that I can't allow myself to be soft. My limits are predetermined. If somebody crosses those limits, my response is automatic. I don't allow myself to think about it.

That ever been tested?

Yes.

And?

If I told you, then I'd be thinking about it.

I guess you would.

She stood to leave, gestured toward the bar.

Would you look at this? she said.

Max was face down on the zinc, the bottle he'd been drinking from spinning empty on its side.

A man his size ought to be able to drink a pond.

I'm sorry, the girl said.

Don't be sorry, be useful. Jonson, see this animal to his room. I don't care if you have to knock him out cold and drag him by the heels—there's nothing in that head you could damage. I'm going to stay and have a chat with his girlfriend.

Jonson lifted Max's head, wiped blood from his lip with a bar rag, then raised him to his feet. Max offered no resistance, made an effort to support his own weight as Jonson steered him across the room.

I ain't a bad man, Max said.

All right.

I ain't.

Sure.

Upstairs, he shied Max onto his bed, switched on the light and shut the door. Without knowing he would, he began to remove Max's boots.

You don't care, Max said. I know you don't.

About what?

Anything.

Is this about those trips?

I could stop her, Max said. Girls and liquor ought to be enough.

Then stop her.

Max coughed, spat a gout of bile onto the floor.

You did what you were told, he said. Get out.

Jonson snicked off the light.

Be smart, Max, he said.

• • •

Jonson took to wandering the upstairs halls, listening. The girls had distinct styles: some screamed as though being riven apart; some bawled commands; some let out slow, spiring moans. Jonson would linger, struggling to supply an image, hearing only pinchbeck affection, overwrought passion, all of it sounding like work. Lying on his cot in the early morning, he would try again, feel nothing.

Once, when Max and the Madame were gone, he took the skeleton key from the bar, tried the Madame's quarters, found them padlocked, moved upstairs to Max's room. Shutting the door behind him, he flicked on the light, eyed the space: a pornographic novel on the nightstand, a bolo knife jutting from under the bed, hummocks of laundry ranging the floor. In the top drawer of the chifforobe, he found a single pair of socks tucked into a ball. He weighed them in his palm, reached his fingers through the tubing, removed a roll of cash wrapped around a chemist's vial. Prodding the vial loose, he lifted it to the light, tilted it forward and back. The cyanic liquid changed hue, darkening as bits of silver dispersed. He uncorked a stopper, breathed in, found no odor. Routing through a pile of laundry, he pulled up a coarse handkerchief, tipped a clean edge into the vial. The liquid permeated a small circle of fabric, seemed to eat away the purple dye.

Jonson sat on the unmade bed, working the stopper back into the vial, the vial into the roll of cash.

She ought to know better, he said aloud. You're too damn dumb for secrets.

VII

The Madame returned from a trip alone.

I need you to stable the horse, she told Jonson.

Where's Max?

Fuck Max.

I don't know anything about...

Learn.

He found the buggy standing crooked on the concrete pathway outside, its bellows top folded down, the footboard scraping the brothel's façade. He circled around, ran his fingers through the horse's mane, slapped the animal's neck.

You been running good, he said.

He walked the horse forward, lifted a match from his front pocket and lit the torches affixed to either side of the forebay door. Shaking the match out, he discovered pinlets of blood cutting sideways across his palm.

You all right there? he asked, patting the horse's muzzle, searching its neck for scrapes or abrasions, finding none.

He picked the reins back up, found patches of still-moist blood spotting the driver's ends, found more blood on and beneath the driver's seat. He unfastened the trace chain, led the horse to its stall, then wiped down the buggy with a burlap rag. He buried the rag and reins in a pile of straw.

Cynthia was waiting up. Jonson peered into the crib, stroked his son's cheek.

I'll do it, Cynthia said.

Do what?

What you asked, she said. If you still want.

I wasn't really asking.

Still.

He sat beside her, bracing his legs to keep the cot from toppling.

I'm not being mean, he said. I just ain't ready.

OK, she said.

It's the truth.

•   •   •

You piece of shit, the Madame said, striking at his form beneath the blanket. Don't you know to wipe a horse down?

What?

He's dead.

Who?

The palomino. You left him lathered. You killed my best horse, you son of a bitch.

Jonson stood, caught her wrists, shook the whip from her hand.

Shut that kid up or I swear to god I'll kill it. I swear to fucking god I will.

Where's Max?

You killed my best horse.

Fuck your horse. Where's Max?

Who?

Max.

What Max? There is no Max. Max is gone.

She was sobbing, convulsing. Jonson backed away, waited for her to finish.

No bar tonight, she said. We're taking a trip.

• • •

It was near dark when they started. The Madame wore
T-bar shoes with diamante trim, a cloche hat. She sat rigid on
the buggy's box, her head angled away from Jonson.

Where are we going? he asked.

Straight until I tell you to turn.

Jonson slackened the reins, urged the surviving horse on.

A car would be faster.

You know I don't ride in cars.

They passed through sparse suburbs, long wooded stretches.
Now and again she took a silverplated flask from her purse and
drank. The working of the reins became automatic. Jonson let
his mind drift, found himself returning to Ray's question: Is this
what she would want?

The Madame guided him onto the lawn of a near-aban-
doned farmhouse, the porch rotting, the paint curling free. She
reached into her purse, pulled out a palm-sized mauser.

Stay here, she said.

You sure?

Don't play brave.

She mounted the porch, entered without knocking. No window came lit. Jonson thought of leaving, of returning for his son
and continuing on, but he couldn't get past the question of where
they would go, and he wasn't sure he could find his way back.

The shots came in quick succession. The horse rose up,
straining to locate the sound.

Hold still, Jonson said.

He jumped down, crouched behind the buggy, grabbed at
the reigns as the horse bucked forward.

Easy now, he said.

The Madame crossed the lawn, settled in the passenger's seat.

I'm done here, she said.

VIII

His son was walking now, keeping to his feet for the length of the basement corridor, the garden pathway. The Madame tended bar herself for a long while, then hired a man whose name Jonson never learned. Soon, the shows would be starting back up. Jonson felt restless, not for the shows themselves, but for the movement, the slow change in scenery as a circuit headed west. The Madame saw it in him.

You've been good to me, she said, sitting beside him at the piano. You're loyal.

I do my job.

You do it with your mouth shut. I want to repay you.

Repay me?

There's someone I want you to meet.

Who's that?

An old friend. I think you can help each other.

OK.

Now, she said.

She led him to a room with bare walls and no windows, a stained-glass chandelier hanging above a round oak table. The silver-haired man with padded shoulders sat opposite the door, rubbing the face of his pocket watch with a silk handkerchief.

How would you like back onstage? he asked.

Jonson turned to the Madame.

I've got reasons, she said.

Doing what? Jonson asked.

Filling out an existing act, the friend said. You can sing? Dance?

I can.

There's more, the Madame said.

More?

More money. More responsibility, the friend said.

How's that?

I've been told you're quiet.

And?

You'd be making deliveries.

Of?

That's what you'd need to keep quiet about.

And my son?

He can stay here, the Madame said. Until he's old enough to be no trouble.

In the basement?

We'll fix up the carriage house for him and Cynthia.

That's one way to make sure I don't talk, he said.

What could you possibly have to talk about? the Madame said. What the hell's wrong with you? We're trying to help.

He thought of Max, wondered if he was now taking the test her nephew had failed.

Nothing, Jonson said. It's good. All of it.

Of course it is, she said.

IX

His bag was packed, the cot folded against a column of boxes.

We'll move the crib into the carriage house, Cynthia said.

He won't need it much longer, Jonson said.

He picked his son up from off her lap, lifted him toward the ceiling.

You won't know who I am next time you see me, he said, then thought: *I'm not sure you know now.*

To Cynthia he said, I guess he's yours.

She took the boy in her arms, raised up on tiptoes, leaned across, kissed Jonson on the cheek. You'll be just fine, Jonson said.

• • •

He boarded the train's center car, took a window seat, slumped down, straddled the valise with the false backing between his legs. He lowered his hat over his eyes, lifted it again once the platform was behind him. He stood, walked to the next car, waited to see if anyone would follow.

The towns became smaller and less frequent, the crops more and more varied. Jonson shut his eyes, felt the fatigue begin to drain from his body, as though he were allowing the train to carry him after days of walking. There was no going back now, he thought. The person he would be was not the person he would have been. He sat up, focused his mind on the career he was returning to rather than the one he had just started. He felt glad to be returning alone.

III

Jonson's Boy

1

It was me who found my father's body and the body of the whore it was tangled up in. The whore's wig was crumpled blond and bloody beside them. Bits of her real hair and skull were mixed with my father's on the plywood bedboard. I spun my head before I saw their faces. I knew it was my father by the scar on his foot where he'd sliced off his own birthmark. There were bruises up and down the whore's legs and I figured it was my father who'd put them there.

The only window in the room was open, the curtains parted and no breeze blowing. I set the whiskey bottle my father had sent me for on the dresser and crossed the room. I bent down, leaned my head outside.

The hotel backed onto the desert. I stayed looking out, listening to the bugs and squinting to catch a lizard or a desert rat darting over the sand or through the scrub. The sun was most of the way down. It was a quiet night, cool and dry with only the stars moving.

I turned around, straining to miss the bed with my eyes. My father's clothes and the whore's clothes were clumped in a pile on the floor. I picked up his pants with my fingertips, went through the pockets and checked inside his shoes. Any money he'd had was gone. His grouch bag was gone and the vials with it. I found the browser's card in an ashtray on the side table. I slid it out, dug it inside my sock. I worked the whiskey bottle into my bag, then stepped to the bed. The sheet was bunched under their feet. I tugged it loose, pulled it over their shoulders and then their heads. Blood soaked into the fabric in uneven circles.

• • •

Outside, I stood on the wooden sidewalk that ran the length of the town's main and only street and tried to make out the time on a clock built into a church steeple, but then I saw that both its hands had broke off. There was a fat man smoking a cigarette and sitting on a stone bench under the hotel's window. I asked him what time it was but he didn't answer. I asked again, but he only coughed out smoke.

I had fifty cents left from when I'd bought the whiskey and that wouldn't get me to New York. The theater hadn't paid us for our turn because my father had fallen from the barrel he was supposed to be dancing on. After he fell he just sat there laughing, his legs spread open and a dark stain growing. Son, your old man ain't worth shit, the manager said. My father laughed all the way through the theater and into the back alley where I thought the manager would beat him, but he just slammed the door. Our lost pay made forty dollars we didn't have.

This time of night the only people on the street had been drinking or were about to be. Some were drinking to be drunk and some were waiting for the late-night train. There was a crowd in front of the bar. One of them was singing and another was dancing to his song. The others watched and laughed. I thought about selling them my bottle but then I thought they'd just take it.

The theater was the last building on the west end of town. I sat on the edge of the wooden curb and practiced what I would say. I picked rocks out of the dirt and tossed them from one hand to the next. I looked in the windows and up the alleys, but there wasn't anybody else around.

I'd start by telling him how much I liked his theater. It's true it was the nicest building in town. The sign above the entrance was hand carved and glazed, with green and yellow leaves painted along the edges. On each side of the entrance door were posters from old shows. Most of the theaters we played look like any other store, flat in front with no decoration. Here, you knew what was waiting inside.

I knocked on the door we'd been thrown out of, but nobody answered. I pulled on the handle, but it wouldn't open. The door was close to the wings and I heard a banjo playing onstage.

I went around to the front and took one of the quarters from my pocket. The woman who sold tickets stopped staring at her magazine long enough to make change. There weren't any words on the page she was reading, just a colorless picture of a falcon with lots of lines and shadows.

Inside, the theater was dark and I had to wait before my eyes could see through the dim light. The banjo player was gone and in his place was a magician who swallowed things and then slid them out of his pockets and sleeves. He swallowed his key, his tie, his shoelace, his gold cufflinks. He asked people in the front row to throw him anything smaller than a cannonball. One woman tossed him a flower and the man she was with stood and handed over his watch. The magician pulled the flower out of his sleeve and the watch out of his breast pocket. When he was done he said, Are you sure you want these back?

The curtain came down and I ran to the front and climbed into the wings. A troupe of acrobats were lined up waiting to tumble onstage. The magician was emptying his pockets into a small canvas bag. I kept walking until I reached the manager's office. He was sitting at his desk, counting bundles of bills and writing out numbers with a long feathery pen.

Jonson's boy, right? he said. You want something?

Yes, sir, I said.

So does everybody.

I don't want much, I said. Just my half.

Half of nothing is nothing, he said. Blame your old man. If I were you, sixteen couldn't come fast enough.

I'm not here about him.

He set down the pen and folded his hands behind his head.

You mean he didn't send you?

No sir. He didn't.

You expect me to believe you came hopscotching over here by your cocksucking little self?

It's the truth.

It's horse shit.

He slid the bundles into an open drawer.

You in trouble, kid?

No.

You sure?

Yeah.

I'll tell you what, he said. Take off your shirt.

What?

Take off your shirt and turn around.

Why?

Consider it a wager. If there aren't welts up and down your spine I'll give you all of it. Yours and your old man's. A wager between men.

He stood and smiled. He kept smiling.

All I want is half, I said.

You'll get all or nothing.

Ten dollars, I said.

I can't help you run away, son.

I'm not your son, I said. I did work for you and now you

have to pay me.

He picked up a silver letter opener that was only a blade with no handle.

Nothing, he said.

. . .

I waited for applause, then made my way back over the stage. I had my hand on the door when I heard a drum roll and more clapping. I turned, saw a boy half my age standing with a melon balanced on his head while his sister aimed her bow and arrow. The girl hit the melon square and split it in two halves that fell slow off her brother's head. The boy reached into a basket and pulled out an apple and held it sideways between his teeth. The girl unsheathed a knife from her belt and without looking flung it so that it stuck in the center of the apple and didn't touch her brother's throat. The boy set aside the knife and the apple and reached back into the basket and came up with as many small oranges as he could fit in his fists. He juggled them and kept them going in the air and the girl took up her bow and arrows and shot them down one by one. I figured his body was scarred from all the times she'd missed.

Outside, the ticket lady was eyeing the same drawing of the same colorless bird. I asked for my quarter back and she looked annoyed like she'd almost had that picture memorized and now she'd have to start over.

We don't hand out money, she said.

But I've got my ticket.

Then you're welcome to go back inside.

You don't understand, I said. I'm in the shows.

Then why'd you buy a ticket?

I thought I had to.

Well then, she said, you learned something.

2

The table cloths were woven like bed spreads and the chairs looked like thrones. The browser sniffed the wine before he let our waiter pour it.

So, what is it we're talking about? my father asked.

A seriocomic of the highest caliber. A flash act with a wow finish. An olio the size of the stages you play now.

Nothing gamy?

In a Pastor establishment?

Tony Pastor?

Yes, sir. Mr. Tony Pastor.

Well now.

Indeed.

The browser turned to me, smiled.

You'd be replacing a son whose voice, at the onset of certain physiological changes, took an unfortunate turn.

Ha, my father said. You mean the kid squeaks.

Not an uncommon phenomenon. But, between us, this development is something of a pretense—the boy was never the strongest link. With a talent such as your son's, they would be looking to expand the part. In fact, there would be a scene in which he held the stage—the full stage—alone. People will notice. Important people. Sir, he said, leaning toward my father,

I've been around since the nickel theaters, and I have seen only a handful—a small handful—of performers as skilled as your boy.

He turned back to me.

I assume you're sixteen? he said. Looking at you now, I might even say seventeen.

He's forty, my father said. Ain't you got nothing for papa?

I have a single income that dwarfs your combined present income.

My father leaned back, grinning.

You talk good, he said, but how do I know you ain't a shine out for attention? Maybe you live down the road.

The browser lowered his fork and knife.

Tell me, he said, who do you follow on your current bill? Who follows you?

A corncob-flute player and an amputee juggler.

Bilge water. At Pastor's, your son will share the stage with a London theater troupe, a concert violinist, people who have played the world's courts. Everything top flight. Can you picture what I'm describing, son?

I could. I saw it now. Faces backlit by the calcium ray. My heels kicking up sawdust.

Here's the thing, my father said. We got obligations.

Obligations?

Things we ain't done with.

You do understand what I'm offering you?

I do. It's generous, my father said. I know it. But the truth is, he ain't sixteen. And he's got some growing left.

But I'm ready now, I said.

I turned before he caught my eyes.

I am offering him an opportunity to grow, the browser said. And if you are worried about the family he will be accompanying, I can assure you...

I said it can wait. The big stage will be there. Right now, he's got a circuit to finish.

The browser let his head drop.

Very principled, he said. But, if I may say so, misguided. Your circuit would not show you the same loyalty. Here's my card. You know where I am staying. I leave for New York in the morning.

• • •

Well, my father said when we were walking back, that was a damn fine meal.

I looked at him. His eyes were red around the rims and he wasn't smiling. He laid a palm on my shoulder.

That man was trying to buy us, he said. We can't be bought. Your turn will come. Soon enough. I promise.

I thought: *Someone bought you.* He saw it in me.

Careful, he said.

I moved away. My body wanted to run. Not toward or from anything. It wanted to let out what I couldn't keep down.

3

The train station was at the far edge of town. I thought I'd trade the whiskey for a ticket, but I didn't want to walk back past the hotel. I pictured faces in the windows watching as my father's naked body was carried off by men I'd never met. There'd be people standing around, the sheriff and the hotel owner and the hotel owner's wife. The wife would tell the sheriff that the man in that room had a boy with him and the sheriff would say he'd find me, only I didn't want to be found.

I passed through an alley, sidled down the embankment that led to the tracks. I could see the station lights the length of the town away. I started walking, counting each track as I went, trying to make out anything that moved. There were things in the desert that could kill you before you knew it, lizards that sidestepped like tiny crabs and cactuses that were so small you couldn't see them.

I heard the growling before I saw the dog. It came out of the brush on the embankment and stood staring at me, its haunches planted and its head down. A shepherd, all bone beneath the fur.

Good boy, I said. Good, good boy.

I bent my knees and slung my bag in front of me. The movement was enough to make him lunge. I hooked my arm through the straps, lifted the bag like a shield and grabbed up a stone. It was almost on me by the time I threw and I saw its mouth turn bloody. I jumped, kicked it solid in the throat, then pelted it with a fistful of rocks while it choked and yelped and dragged itself back to where it came from.

A man stepped out of the scrub and stood facing me so I couldn't pass. He was tall and ugly, dressed in a ragged slicker with boots that ran to his knees. He had a whip coiled in one hand and I could tell by the dog that he knew how to use it.

That animal's worth money, he said.

It'll live, I said.

But it's broken. Damaged. I expect to be compensated.

You set that dog to kill me.

What's in your bag?

Nothing.

The bag itself is something.

The bag itself is mine.

You'll leave here in better shape than my dog if you give it to me.

He let out some slack on the whip.

I didn't mean to hurt him, I said.

He cocked his arm.

That's odd, he said. I thought you did.

I thought he'd hit me, but he only called to the dog while it whimpered and crawled towards him. He set down his whip, grabbed the dog's neck and pointed at its bloody mouth.

You see, he said. You knocked away the animal's bite.

And this, he said. He took the dog's paw between his fingers and pressed until it screamed.

You caught him on the foot, he said. Broken. He's no good for travel now. What would you have me do with a lame dog?

Who put those scars on its back? I asked.

Awful brazen, son, he said. But brazen won't save you. He

127

slapped the dog's rump, shooed it back into the scrub.

I'll take my goods, he said.

I started to run, but he snaked my ankle. I landed hard on my side and the whip slashed my cheek. I tucked my knees to my chest while he wailed on my back. Then I lay on the tracks wishing for the train.

•   •   •

I pushed myself up, saw the man was gone and my bag wasn't. He hadn't taken the bottle. I climbed the embankment and headed for the town. The windows in the buildings were black now. My back was burning and I could tell from the way my face ached that I needed to clean the wound. I hopped from one sidewalk to the other, then peered into the bar. Stepping in from the unlit street my eyes saw purple and then they cleared and I made out a room of faces, all of them looking like my old man on a good day before the liquor turned him sour.

Shit, kid, the bartender said. You want a doctor?

All I want is water, I said.

He picked up a pitcher and poured me a glass, then spilled some water onto a clean rag and passed the rag to me. I held the damp cloth against my cheek.

Who did that to you, son? a man asked.

I didn't answer.

Somebody did it to you.

I walked to the bar, dragging my foot to cover my limp.

Was it your old man? the bartender asked. He had rotted-out teeth and a scar where part of an ear was gone. I took the water and drank it.

My old man ran off, I said.

After he did that to you?

I did it to myself, I said.

Why?

I didn't say anything. I sat on a stool at the bar with my back to the room. Some of them thought I was lying to protect my old man, and some of them thought I was lying for reasons they didn't know.

That's the singer, one of them said. That's the kid whose father was tight onstage.

Was your old man tight? the bartender asked. Did he cut you when he was tight?

He didn't cut me.

Someone said, I wish my kid would lie like that for me.

I'm hungry, I said.

We have sandwiches, the bartender said. But you'll have to pay for food.

I can sing for it, I said.

The bartender smiled.

You sure you feel up to it?

I nodded. He pointed to a piano buried under empty glasses along the far wall.

You play, Nick.

Nick can't see straight.

I'm fine, Nick said.

He's fine, someone else said.

I need more water, I said.

The bartender emptied his pitcher into my glass.

And a quarter a song, I said.

The crowd behind me started to laugh.

Hey, someone said. I'm starting to think whoever cut him got the worse end of things.

Shut your mouth, the bartender said. Here's your first quarter, son.

I buried it in my sock. Nick sat and played through a few

scales. The notes sounded like a thin stick knocking against an empty tin. People applauded and hollered like I was taking the stage. The bartender passed around a bottle. Nick started up an old ballad about a covered wagon and a gold mine and the folks who died along the way. It was slow with the notes all close together. A few bars in, my cheek opened. I tried to rush the words, but Nick was already behind. When I finished, the men threw pennies at my feet. Some of them threw dimes.

You're bleeding pretty bad there, Nick said.

I touched my cheek. Blood came off thick on my fingers.

I need to wash.

Show the kid the jon, the big one said.

This way, son. The bartender stepped out from behind the bar and led me down a small hallway. He pushed open a door, stood watching.

I have to do more than wash, I said.

I slid the lock in place, then started the water. There was a small, boat-style window cut into the pine wall. It opened inward, with a metal chain running from the frame to the wall so that the window could only open so far. I tried to pull the chain loose from the wall but the nail had been hammered deep into the wood. I looked for something to pry the nail free, but the bathroom was just a toilet and a sink and cracked tile on the floor. Outside, the bartender coughed to let me to know he was still there. I splashed some water in the sink and turned the faucet off and on. I cursed my father for pawning his knife—a hunter's knife with an ivory handle and a thick blade that came to a fine point.

I flipped through some pennies looking for a flattened edge. There was a dime mixed in and I thought it might be thin enough to wedge between the nail and wood. I tried to scrape shavings from the pine around the nail's head but I couldn't push through the shellac. I bent my knees and straightened my back against the wall, trying for a better look at the window's frame. The wood there was untreated and some of it had been eaten through by bugs. It gave a little when I dug in with the dime, but I had to keep my arms at an angle and the dime slipped from my fingers and bounced against the tiles. The bartender knocked on the door and asked if I was all right. I said I'd be fine, but my stomach was sick. He said something else I didn't hear. I pressed my palms flat against the window's frame, pushed until my elbows locked and the chain came free.

What was that? the bartender asked.

I'm gonna puke, I said. I made noises like I was about to be sick and for a while I believed I was.

I went to the sink. The basin had cracked and the crack had filled with grime. There wasn't any soap. I lowered my head, let the water flood my cheek. The basin turned red. I shut off the faucet, plugged the cut with toilet paper.

Open the door, kid, the bartender said.

I need to cool off, I said. I crammed the words full of my breath.

The toilet water was yellow from the last man to piss in it. I tugged on the chain. I pulled hard and the water started to swirl and while it did I threw my bag out the window and then stepped on the rim with my good foot and pushed myself up and through.

4

I made my way toward the station, leaning against the buildings when my ankle gave. I kept looking back, but if someone were after me they'd have found me by now, hopping and limping and sweating like I was. I felt bugs landing and pushing off on my face. I slapped myself up and down but didn't kill a thing.

At the end of the street, I saw the hotel and the station behind it. No one was gathered out front. They hadn't found the bodies. If I'd wanted to, I could have walked up the stairs and into the room. I could have slept on the cot with my father and the whore lying quiet beside me.

Even with the dimes and the last quarter I didn't have more than two dollars and some cents. I folded the coins in the bill and clamped the bill in my fist. The depot was empty except for an old man standing in a wooden booth with metal bars for a window. A chalkboard outside listed the stops the train would make and the miles to each one. The old man didn't look at me when I walked up. I thought either he was blind or asleep.

I don't have enough money, I said.

Then I don't have enough tickets, he said.

But I do have something, I said. I pulled out the whiskey and set it on the counter.

Sober twenty years, he said.

You could sell it.

Got a job.

There was a scratched-up shotgun leaning against the wall behind him. The light bulb hung an inch from his scalp.

I've got two dollars, I said. Where can I go for two dollars?

Anywhere you can walk, he said. He laughed, like someone else had told the joke.

I'll work, I said. I'll carry people's suitcases. I'll stay in the back with the baggage.

You sound like a young man in trouble. I feel for you, he said. But I can't help you.

He was half-smiling like he'd gone back to thinking about whatever had been on his mind before I cut in. I walked outside and stood in the dark. I crouched, spit into the ground, scrubbed the wet dirt over my hands. I ran my fingers through my hair, across my shirt, down the uncut side of my face.

I sat on the ground outside the station door. I tried sitting like I had no life left in me. I slouched against the wall, but the wood was rough on my scabs. I slumped forward, felt my skin spread until the cuts opened back up. I took off my shoe and set it in front of me with the mouth pointed up. I rested my head in my hands, one palm cupped over my cut cheek. I sat that way for a long while. Nobody came. My eyes started to shut.

I woke to heels grinding down on the gravel. I lifted my shoe and, without thinking I would, started to sing. I sang the first song I'd learned, a nursery rhyme my father danced to in an act that had me dressed like a school boy with a bow tie and collar and pants that ended just below my knees. In the act, my father was walking me to school and I was singing the reasons I didn't need to go. It started as a duet, with me singing the things I knew already and him answering with the things I didn't. I know my abc's. But what about your d's through z's? After a while he gave up answering and just danced.

I sang both our parts, slower and sadder than we had on stage. I hung my chin low and raised the shoe over my head. People were hurrying to meet the train, but some of them stopped. There was a man who'd strapped his bags to a dolly but the wheels caught in the gravel and the bags fell over. He righted them and pulled them farther and it happened again. He sat on his fallen bags and listened. He was only resting but I didn't care because when he got up he stuffed a dollar in my shoe.

A pregnant woman with skinny arms dropped in fifty cents and the man with her dropped in another quarter. A group of show folk carrying instruments applauded and took up a collection. By the time I heard the train coming I had enough for a ticket and a sandwich too.

I rubbed the dirt from my face and ran into the station and slid the fare under the metal bars. The old man didn't seem to remember me. He counted the money as slow as he could, then slapped his hands together and tore off my ticket. I walked out onto the platform with the people who'd paid my way.

The conductor blew the train's whistle but I didn't step back. A man in a bell-top hat greeted people and took their tickets. I stood close enough to the show folk that he might think I was with them. They filled his palm, then mounted the steps with their instruments strapped to their backs.

You by yourself, son? he asked.

He shut his fist. His hair was black above his lip and gray where it curled from under his hat.

I'm sixteen, I said.

Who did that to you? he asked. He asked it quick like it wasn't worth saying he didn't believe me, then stepped off the train and looked up and down the platform.

I got separated from my father, I said.

Separated how? he asked.

I didn't say anything.

Tell me what happened, he said.

I have family in Chicago, I said.

They'll have to come for you, he said.

But you don't understand, I said.

And I don't have time to.

He stepped back onto the train.

But I have a ticket, I said.

Doesn't matter, he said.

What do you mean?

Nothing's going to happen on my train.

It won't, I said. I promise.

If you could keep your promises you wouldn't look like that, he said.

He leaned out of the door and gestured as if he were chopping wood.

Please, I said.

The train started moving, slow, as though it might stall under the added weight. I watched it stutter past, watched the gears drawing circles and the faces looking at me through the windows. The last face I saw was pressed against the glass and at first I thought the flattened features belonged to the man with the whip but then they were gone and I couldn't be sure.

I turned back toward the depot. The lights were out. The old man was gone and so was my money.

5

If you were expecting someone younger, I must say I was expecting someone older. Just what is your age?

Fifteen, I said.

I might have believed thirteen, she said. No matter. Please, sit.

We sat with a tray of food between us—bowls of olives, a plate of cheese, a pitcher of tea. Her apartment was a single room with a stove in one corner and a bed in the other. She'd arranged vases of flowers on the table, the window sills, the floor, the stove. I set the bag on the tray.

She smiled.

It's a cruel world, she said. You know what is inside that bag?

Yes ma'am.

You have lovely manners.

She raised a fist to her mouth, tried to hold down a cough that in the end came rushing up, long and loud and deep. Her eyes watered. She reached for a handkerchief.

I am dying, she said. My doctor tells me that, in the months to come, I will forget things. Things I've always known. I will hallucinate. I'll lose control of my functions. I'll be in constant agony from head to toe. I haven't lived a perfect life, but I believe I merit a better end.

She opened the bag, pulled out a vial.

Have you tried it? she asked.

No ma'am.

Are you lying?

No ma'am.

I'm told it can produce a kind of euphoria. A calm settles in. After a while, you simply go blank. Would you agree that this sounds like a better exit than the one my doctor described?

Yes, ma'am. I would.

Good, she said. I was worried that I might frighten you— that you might try to talk me out of it. Tell me, where are your parents?

My father's at the hotel.

And your mother?

She's dead.

Did you know her?

No.

A pity. Tell me, as my final wish, will you make me one promise?

All right.

Promise me that when you're old enough, you'll strive for something good. What you're doing now is beneath you, but you're not to blame. As soon as you can, you must hold yourself to a higher standard. Will you make me that promise?

Yes ma'am.

Wonderful. Now, I would like for you to stay with me while I make the preparations.

I watched her draw the shades, paint her eyes and cheeks, dab her neck with perfume. She took an envelope from a drawer in her dresser, leaned it against a vase on the table. She filled a tall glass with expensive-looking liquor, drank it a quarter down, then filled it again with what was in the vials. She set the glass on her nightstand.

You see, she said, that I am not frightened either?

Yes.

It is good for you to see that. Now, will you kindly start the phonograph on your way out?

The needle stuck a bit. I picked it up and set it down farther along. The music was all piano, the notes running high and low. I heard her choke behind me. I looked back. The glass was empty. She was lying with her hands folded over her stomach. Her lace dress matched the bedspread.

6

I hobbled along the backs of the buildings until I found a fire escape that was built like a staircase instead of a ladder. I sat on the bottom step with my leg stretched forward and started backward up the stairs, pressing down on my palms to lift my weight onto the step behind me. The wood was rough like it had warped after a long rain. Splinters dug into my skin.

The roof was covered with gravel. Someone had stacked broken furniture and crates of empty bottles and old newspapers along the edge closest to the street. Mixed in amongst the trash was a rocking chair with the backing busted out and a half-shredded blanket draped across the arms. I set down my bag and crawled over the gravel, careful not to wake whoever was sleeping beneath me.

I spread the blanket open, then took the whiskey out of my bag and used the bag as a pillow. I lay on my side because I couldn't lay on my back. There wasn't a sound anywhere. No bugs, no birds, no breeze or music, no traffic starting and stopping on the street below me.

I lay there for a long while with nothing to do but think. I could have thumbed down a truck and been a hundred miles to New York by now. I could have dared the manager to cut me, then stood there until he gave me money to go away. I could have fought off the man with the whip the way I'd fought off his dog. I could have asked the musicians at the station to hire me on.

I reached for the bottle, uncapped it and took a long swallow. I took one more, then shut my eyes.

I dreamt my father was alive. The whore was alive too, only she wasn't a whore, just a woman who lived with us in a large house with wood floors and lots of windows. I had a fever so high it hurt to open my eyes. There were blankets over me and a wet cloth on my forehead. The woman sat beside me where I lay on the couch, shushing me, smiling down at me, telling me to be quiet and rest, only I wasn't talking.

It's OK, she said. We'll sort it out when you're well.

I wanted to ask, Sort what out? but my tongue was swollen and I couldn't get the words around it. My father came up behind her.

I thought she told you to be quiet, he said.

It's all right, the woman said.

It isn't, my father said. To me he said, Shut your mouth. And quit your goddamned thrashing.

He pushed the woman away, leaned over me, pinned my arms to the cushion.

Shut up, he said.

He slapped my face, then lifted me up and let me fall. I turned my head, trying to stifle my mouth in the pillow, but I couldn't reach. I felt the bruises turning dark on my arms. He slapped me again. I looked up at him. There was blood pouring from his nose and I could see his cheek bones where patches of skin had rotted off.

Shut your mouth, he said.

The woman disappeared behind him.

7

I was all the way asleep when my father came back. He rocked me by the shoulder.

I got an idea, he said.

He was laughing. I could smell the liquor on him.

We're gonna cut off your hands. Both of them. It's got to be both cause one's been done already.

He dropped back on his bed, still laughing.

We'll be rich, he said. It's sure fire.

I rolled onto my side, folded a pillow over my head but didn't sleep. After a while, I sat up. His snoring was hard and broken.

I crouched by the window, thumbed a stopper from a vial and tapped a third of the liquid onto the rag my father used. I rubbed the damp patch of cloth over my gums.

I stood, pacing, then lay back down. I felt a rush of heat like when the curtain first rises and the lights hit your face, and then it passed and I was on the deck of a boat, leaning over the railing, looking into the water. Deep in the water I saw buildings made of piano keys and trees with human hands for leaves. But then the boat stopped moving and the water kept on so that the images blurred, and then I sat up and vomited all over my bedding. My vision went blank, and for a long while there was only sickness.

. . .

I woke to my father's laughing. I saw him standing over me, his eyes turning liquid, and I heard him say, You stupid ass. He said it again and again. A week's supply, he said. He laughed himself breathless.

I fell back asleep and when I woke again it was night and my sheet and blanket were gone.

You all right now? he asked.

I'm hungry.

That it?

I rubbed my eyes, nodded.

Get up, he said.

He pulled off his belt, wrapped the buckled end around one hand.

Besides the supply, we lost a booking, he said. And I owe the hotel for the bedding.

I won't do it again.

I doubt you will. But I got to make sure.

The blows felt like I was being punched instead of whipped.

8

The sun was up, but barely. I tried to stand, but my ankle wouldn't hold my weight. I kneeled and pissed in a corner, then packed the blanket into my bag. I thought about the bundles of cash in the manager's office. Once I thought of them I couldn't think of anything else. I started down the fire escape. My shoe caught in the bottom rung and I tripped and fell. The rocks tore my shirt at the elbow and I laughed out loud thinking what I must look like hobbling around with my cut up face and hands and legs.

The street was empty. I made my way to the theater, tried the side door, then walked to the back. The first floor windows were too high for me to reach, but there were smaller windows just above the ground that looked into the cellar. I lay on my side and kicked out a pane of glass with my good foot, then reached in and slid open the latch that held the frame closed. Bits of glass had scattered across the cellar floor. I turned onto my stomach with my bag strapped to my back, slid my body down.

The cellar was crowded with coat racks and boxes of playbills and broken seats. There were stained drop cloths and used and unused brushes and dented cans of paint. There were sealed crates piled to the ceiling. There was just enough space cleared for me to walk through.

I used the railing like a crutch, came out in a corridor with no windows or light. I felt along the wall for the switch.

I listened at the manager's door, then turned the handle. He kept it locked. I pushed as hard as I could without falling down, but the door wouldn't give. I got on my knees and took off my belt. I'd seen my father pick a lock with the tongue part of his buckle. He just stuck it in the keyhole and flicked it around until something clicked. I worked the metal up and down and side to side until the lock gave.

I opened the drawer where he'd pushed in the bundles, then opened the drawer under it, and the drawer under that. They were full of partly smoked cigars, open match boxes with burned out matches stuck back inside, marked up programs, sealed jars of ink, some coins that I pocketed, a half-sandwich wrapped in newsprint with the butter melted through. The bundles were gone.

I hopped along the edges of the room, knocking the posters from the walls. I rapped my knuckles over the sides of his desk, but the wood was solid. I sat back down in his chair, pulled the drawers out one by one and dumped their insides on the floor. I got on my hands and knees. Amongst the coins and scraps of paper were two silver-blue vials. I dropped them into my pocket, pushed myself back up.

I took the half-sandwich off the floor and unwrapped it. The paper stained my fingers with grease and ink. There were words imprinted on the bread. I scraped the bread clean with his letter opener, wiped the blade on my pants and slid it into my bag. I ate the sandwich faster than I could taste it.

There was a fresh cigar lying on his desk. I lit it and stuck the end between my teeth. I picked up my bag.

I turned the lights on over the stage and the gallery. There was a painting on the ceiling that I hadn't seen before, an eagle perched in a tree above a deep ravine. I sat on the edge of the boards near the center, turning the cigar in my fingers and squinting at the eagle until I made its wings flap with my eyes.

Standing with the cigar in my mouth, I pulled the whiskey from my bag. Ashes blew down and stuck to my shirt. I slapped them away, then walked to the back of the stage and emptied the bottle in long streaks up and down the curtain. The red turned dark under the liquor. I held the lit end of the cigar to the damp fabric, watched the curtain catch flame.

I sat on the wooden sidewalk, waiting, rubbing my thumb over the raised lettering on the browser's card. The sun was up now. It wasn't long before the bell sounded in the steeple and kept sounding. Men ran past, one at a time and then in packs. Some of them were dressed in their night clothes. They came with buckets and shovels and blankets. I could smell the burning. I could see the flames breaking through the top of the theater.

Women and children hurried by. I walked up the street, fingering the vials in my pocket. Soon, everyone in town had gathered around the theater. There was a wood-bodied stake truck parked outside the general store. Lettering on the driver's door read Wool's Brewery, Denver Colo. The bed was empty save for a crumpled canvas tarp. I crawled under it, laid on my back as flat as I could. The canvas stunk of malt and something sour. The planks were hard against my spine. Before long, the cab door slammed and the bed started to vibrate. The wheels kicked dustspurs up between the slats. I cupped my palms over my nose and mouth. I didn't know how far we were or if we'd make it in a single day. Denver was more town than city, but it had a real station with major lines passing through. I'd sell the vials for a ticket and a new set of clothes. I'd telegraph Mr. Murry to say I was coming.

IV

THE INSPECTOR

I

He could see the town emerging some miles distant, the wooden frames appearing as a break in the brush and scrub. He lifted his handkerchief from the steering wheel, wiped sweat off his forehead, his neck, from between the folds of his stomach. Pulling part way off the road, he left the motor running while he relieved himself into the hard sand. Antelope stopped and stared; he clapped his hands, watched them scatter.

He drove on, thinking through his final conversations with Jonson, searching for any indication that Jonson might have tipped his hand. The Inspector had been clear with him: no letters, no telegrams; a single phone call after each delivery, never from the hotel or theater. If Jonson had been discovered, then it was unlikely that the supply remained in town. But it was too soon to speculate. Jonson had been ill-humored, intemperate. Anyone might have found motive to kill him.

•   •   •

The hotel owner and his wife sat a foot apart on a stone bench, looking as if neither had spoken for some time. They were old, their bodies eroded, the skin dried tight over their bones. The Inspector observed them from inside his car, reached behind and pulled a black bag off the back seat. He cut the ignition, waited for the engine to cease sputtering.

You the Inspector? the owner called, attempting to stand.

I am, the Inspector answered. Do you own this place?

I do. And I need them bodies gone.

Awful business, the wife said. Awful, awful business.

You'll want a room, she added.

I'll see the bodies first.

He followed the owner through an unadorned lobby and up a narrow flight of stairs, into a long corridor lined on both sides with closely spaced doors. The Inspector stopped, tapped the wall with his ring finger, listened as the sound passed through.

Nobody heard the shots? he asked.

We get mostly show folk, the owner said. And most of them was at the theater or out getting something to eat. If it happened later, when they was asleep, they would've heard it. Unless they was all drunk, which ain't unlikely.

What about you?

Don't drink.

Did you hear the shots?

Me and the missus got a room in the basement. Can't hear a thing down there, which is how we like to live.

He unlocked a door, pushed it open, stepped aside to let the Inspector pass. The curtains were parted, the window cracked. The Inspector set down his bag and pulled out a pair of gloves.

Gonna poke around a bit?

That cot belonged to the boy?

Yes sir. Ain't seen him since. Maybe it was him who done it. Or maybe he's kidnapped.

Did you pull this sheet over them?

No sir. Found them like that.

And the second victim?

She wasn't with them when they checked in.

Has anyone else seen the bodies?

One who shot them, I suppose. We ain't had law here since our sheriff died.

You should leave now, the Inspector said. I'll be down to ask more questions.

Can I call the undertaker?

Best wait until I'm done.

All right, Inspector. But don't dally. My wife don't like having them bodies on our property.

He heard the hotel keeper's footsteps receding down the hallway, heard the stairs creaking under his slight weight. He walked to the window, leaned his head outside. No fire escape, no ladder. He ran his fingers along the untreated wood beneath the sill, checking for abrasions, indentations, an indication that someone had come and gone in a hurry. But the wood was clean, as was the ground below—no tire treads, no broken scrub, nothing but the immediate beginning of the desert interrupted a short way off by train tracks, then desert again for as far as his vision would carry.

He turned from the window, stepped to the bed. The fabric conformed to their bodies, the blood having pasted it down about their heads. He took the edges of the sheet between his thumbs and forefingers, peeled it back, revealing a girl on top, Jonson underneath, her fingers gripping his ears, his arms wrapped tight around the small of her back. The shooter stood directly above them, fired twice into the back of the girl's skull. The Inspector knelt down, pinched a lock of the girl's hair and gently raised her head. The first bullet had stuck in her skull, the second passed through and pierced her client's eye. He shifted her head to the side, lifted Jonson's, found that the second bullet had likewise exited his skull and lodged just below the surface of the mattress. He dug it out with his penknife, dropped it into his left jacket pocket.

He ran his eyes down the girl's body. There were multiple contusions on the back of each leg, all of uniform shape and size, the spacing between them near exact. He took a ruler from his bag, measured the length and width of each bruise, then measured Jonson's fingers, his palms, the backs of his hands. No match. He lifted Jonson's belt from the floor, spread it across the girl's legs: at its thinnest point it would have left a wider, fatter mark.

He rolled the girl onto her back so that her head lay cradled in the crux of her client's arm. She was plump, pale, and—judging by the smoothness and firmness of her skin, the size and shape of her breasts—between the ages of sixteen and eighteen. The wounds were such that he could not determine the color of her eyes.

Her mouth, however, remained intact, her teeth clamped tight, as if she'd faced her death by biting down. He parted her lips, inserted his thumbs and forefingers, prized the jaws open. The papillae around the necks of her bottom teeth were stained blue—a pure, bright hue. He lifted her tongue, found the frenulum similarly discolored, the stains coming in brighter, wider patches. The discoloration had progressed further in Jonson's mouth, where that same shade had overtaken stretches of vascular membrane, had crept up through the frenulum and into the tongue itself.

Both victims were tattooed: the girl bore a large butterfly on her inner-thigh, meant to hide a series of small, circular burns; Jonson wore his name traced in black script across the base of his neck, low enough to cover with a collar or scarf.

The Inspector turned from the bodies, opened and closed the empty dresser drawers. Kneeling, he pulled a bag from beneath the bed, scattered its contents across the floor. Anything of value was gone. In his final report, Jonson claimed to have a quarter of his supply remaining. If that were true, then either the killer or the boy had taken those vials. If the boy had taken them, it meant he knew their worth, which in turn meant that he might be able to corroborate his father's account.

. . .

The hotel owner's wife stood behind the counter, her face framed by a pegboard key rack, her expression vacant as she filed thick sheets of paper into a long tin box.

A word with you? the Inspector said.

Just a moment, she said. She fingered the papers in front of her, furrowing her brow as though he'd broken her concentration. The Inspector leaned across the counter, lifted the lid and set it softly in place, forcing her to withdraw her hands.

A word, he said, pulling out his notebook.

Certainly, she said.

The boy? he said.

The boy, she said, was between twelve and fourteen years of age, wiry, sallow, tall, hair unkempt, clothes this side of threadbare. He was not well looked after, but then the father did not look after his own self. The father she described as the remains of a man who had once been handsome, whose blue eyes had lost their focus, whose chest had all but collapsed, whose bones pressed through his flesh. His speech was not slurred, but somehow altered. The boy, she continued, seemed deferential, indifferent, *like a prisoner in mid-sentence.*

The Inspector nodded, pocketed his notebook.

Obliged, he said.

Inspector, she said, leaning forward, would you like your room now?

Not just yet.

He turned to leave, saw a man standing in the door frame,

his face and clothes coated with soot.

Mavis, the man called, moving past the Inspector, I'm looking for a piece of shit named Jonson. Has a boy with him.

Mavis said nothing. The Inspector pivoted, distinguished the butt of a gun protruding from the man's pants.

What room, Mavis?

The Inspector took a quick stride, snatched the gun with one hand, grabbed the man's bicep with the other.

Hold on, he said.

I'll crack your goddamned skull.

With what? I have your gun.

This is the Inspector, Mavis said: smiling, nervous.

What are you inspecting?

Murder, Mavis said.

Thank you, Mavis, the Inspector said. I'll take it from here.

Whose murder?

The Inspector emptied the chamber, set the gun and bullets on the counter. He lifted a single bullet up to the light, removed the slug from his jacket pocket.

What the hell is this?

I'm guessing it was your theater that burned down?

Yeah. I'm the manager anyway. And I know damn well who did it.

Who's that?

That drunk and his boy.

Doubtful.

How's that?

The drunk is dead. Murdered. Sometime last night.

Mavis, that true?

Oh, yes, said Mavis.

Let's talk, the Inspector said. The manager gathered his gun and bullets, trailed the Inspector outside.

Sit, the Inspector said, gesturing to the stone bench beneath the hotel's window.

What about the boy? the manager asked. Where's the boy?

Please sit, the Inspector said.

This ain't your office.

We could use yours, if you like.

It was that boy burned down my theater. You find him before I do.

I'm going to sit, the Inspector said.

Then fucking sit.

Now, the Inspector said, sitting, you seem convinced the fire was set deliberately.

Is that a question?

It is.

It's a fool one.

Answer it just the same.

The boy must have murdered his old man. It'd be a hell of a coincidence otherwise—two crimes that big in a single night.

I'm not sure that the boy did murder his father.

Then you're good for shit.

All I know for certain is that the boy is missing. And you came here thinking that either he or his father set the fire. But Jonson is dead.

If you're going to ask a question, ask it.

All right. What made you think that either of them had set the fire?

They were trash.

And?

The father fell down drunk onstage. The boy tried to make like it was part of the act, but everybody knew.

So you had them removed?

I removed them myself.

Did they put up a fight?

Not then. The father had pissed himself. Couldn't stop laughing.

When?

When what?

Did they put up a fight?

They didn't. But the boy came back later.

By himself?

Yeah, by himself.

How much later?

It was night. Ten, maybe eleven o'clock.

Go on.

He wanted his half.

Was he carrying his belongings?

He had a bag slung over his shoulder. At first I figured his old man put him up to it, but then I figured he was running off. If he did do in his old man it was a mercy killing.

Good for shit, was he?

Less than shit. Can I go now?

Yes, though I'd like to know where.

To find the boy.

It would be better for everyone if you left that to me.

Is that an order?

If you like.

He watched the manager walk away, soot shaking free from his thighs, his shadow dragging the ground behind him. He climbed into a pickup truck, the bed crowded with scorched lumber, turned the ignition and took off through town.

• • •

Throughout the initial interrogation, Jonson held to the story his employers had scripted: a man he met on an overnight train gave him fifty dollars to make the delivery and promised the buyer would pay him twice that amount.

What was his name?

He never said.

What did he look like?

It was dark, and we had a flask.

What exactly is in the vials?

You'd have to ask the man on the train.

The Inspector changed tacks, turned his questions to Jonson's life outside of the vials. Over time, Jonson became more responsive, though his answers seldom spilled into a second sentence. He was a widower, a father, a showman. He had no permanent residence, no account in any bank. He and his son spent summers performing up and down the eastern shore; fall through spring, they toured with whatever circuit would have them. His son was the real talent. The stage, for Jonson, was more job than calling.

And how long do you and your son spend at each stop on the circuit?

Sometimes one night. Sometimes a full week.

So you're on the road quite a bit?

More than we're onstage.

Is that why they picked you?

Who?

Whoever manufactures the vials?

You'd have to ask the man on the train.

Ultimately, it was nothing the Inspector said or did but rather the passage of time that caused a change in Jonson's demeanor. By late afternoon, his voice took on a strained quality, his neck broke out in colorless hives, he appeared suddenly more frail.

Why don't we rest for a moment? the Inspector said.

He returned a short while later with a cup of coffee for himself, a glass of water for Jonson.

I have the impression, he said, that someone gave you bad advice. I think they told you that if you insisted on a lie there was nothing anyone could do to you. Let me tell you what I can do. I can keep you until you say something I believe. My work day ends in a quarter hour. Once those fifteen minutes are up, I'll have an officer show you to your cell, and we will begin again in the morning.

I told you what I know.

We'll see.

Let me get word to my son.

We will speak with him for you. Does he have anyone he can stay with?

He can stay with himself.

If you feel he's safe.

You know, Jonson said. You ain't said one thing I believe, either.

Is that so?

Fifteen minutes from now you got no place to be. No wife. No kids. No one but the people you talk to in this room, and they don't tell you a goddamn thing you want to hear.

About your boy, the Inspector said. How can we reach him?

• • •

The sun struck his skin as though it were standing next to him. He loosened his tie, undid the top button of his shirt, slung his jacket over his shoulder. He stood with his back arched, surveying the street, taking slow note of the facades, the signboards, the cars parked perpendicular to the wooden sidewalks. The buildings were all two stories tall, the ground floor for commerce, the top for lodging. At present, he was the only person in view.

He came first to the general store. The door was propped open with a sack of flour; strings of red peppers and links of sausage hung in the windows. The man behind the counter was busy prodding something with a stick, the object hidden from view behind jars of candy and stacked pouches of tobacco. The Inspector stepped further into the store, saw that the shopkeeper was not prodding, but rather stuffing a large, dead bird—some sort of desert buzzard with brindled wings and a long, black beak—with balls of cotton that he kept in a bucket on the counter. The bird was mounted, belly up, on a tri-partite pedestal made expressly for the purpose, perhaps expressly for this bird, with three u-shaped prongs meant to cradle the buzzard's neck, back, and talons respectively. The deep wooden shelves behind the shopkeeper housed desert creatures of all species, preserved in every conceivable posture: a rat, tail raised, lips curled, incisors shining—perhaps polished or even painted—poised to fight, presumably its last fight; a coyote pup, ears flopped forward, body twisted, hind leg raised to scratch a flea or tick or whatever insect might itch in the desert; a jack rabbit flat on its back, one ear dangling off the shelf; a small wildcat slapping the air with its paw. The poses did not so much preserve the dead as they did a moment of living, or, as with the jack rabbit, the first moment of death. The Inspector cleared his throat, nodded, received no reply.

He walked the aisles, making sure the boy was not there, stopping to finger a box of cigars, to note the prices of the canned goods. He returned to the counter, held out his badge.

What can I do for you? the shopkeeper asked. He removed his blood-stained gloves, tucked them into his apron pocket, extended his hand.

You're quite the craftsman, the Inspector said.

If you call it craft, the shopkeeper said. It makes the day go by. Not a lot of traffic here in the afternoons.

I can imagine, the Inspector said.

Preserve them with my own concoction. I'm working on a patent.

Is this your shop?

Nope. I just run it.

A question.

Yes, sir.

I'm looking for a boy. He'd be on his own, between twelve and fourteen, tall for his age either way.

This about that fire?

Possibly, the Inspector said. Possibly not.

Well, he was in here, the shopkeeper said. Last night, right before I closed. Came in and bought a bottle of whiskey. Had a signed note said it was for his old man.

What was the boy like? His manner?

Didn't really have one. Don't think he said a word. Just gave me the note.

One more thing, the Inspector said. A sign outside says you handle the mail.

I do. This town ain't big enough for a proper post office.

Would you still have today's?

Outgoing, I would. Leaves every second evening.

Mind if I take a look?

Is that legal?

This is a federal investigation.

Does that answer my question?

It does.

All right, I won't stand in your way.

He slid the bird up the counter, lifted a wickerwork basket from the floor and set it before the Inspector. Inside were a half-dozen letters.

You might be able to help me, the Inspector said, removing the envelopes from the basket, laying them out on the counter with the addresses facing the shopkeeper. Could you tell me which of these were posted by residents of this town and which by visitors?

The shopkeeper spread his palms on the counter, transferred his gaze from one envelope to the next.

They don't all have return addresses, he said. People are lazy that way.

Yes, but as the postman in a town this size, you must have an idea of who the locals correspond with. Are any of these addressees unfamiliar?

Whoever you're looking for ain't local?

No, though they may have been here a week or two already.

They?

Yes.

Well, there is one jumped out at me. He tapped a creased envelope with his ring finger. We don't get much headed for New York.

To his surprise, the Inspector recognized the slanting, over-sized scrawl. Jonson had not seemed the type to keep in touch.

Obliged, he said, folding the envelope into his jacket pocket.

Ain't you going to read it?

Yes.

But not now?

I thank you for your time.

To Mr. Murry—

It was hard thinking of my boy on the boards without me. I needed time and now I had it. We have this one circuit to finish. I know you said this was a one time thing and it was now or not at all but we both know if your offer don't stand another one will. I will have him in NY before Xmas.

From—
X

The Inspector folded the letter in uneven thirds, returned it to his pocket, then stood scanning the shops on the opposite side of the street. At a little before dinner time, only the saloon was open. He crossed, pushed his way through the swinging shutters. There were five or more men seated at the bar, each a stool apart, drinking beer and eating peanuts, smoking, pretending not to notice the Inspector's entrance. A lone woman sat at the far end, inhaling from a cigarette that had burned most of the way down. The Inspector took the stool beside her, laid open his wallet and tapped his badge.

A word, he said.

Perkes? she called. An outsized bartender stepped forward, a man whose blunt features seemed like place holders marking where more permanent features might some day be grafted on.

Your name is Perkes? the Inspector said.

It is, Perkes answered.

Do you own this place?

Just work the bar.

And you are? the Inspector asked the woman.

Audrey, she said.

Audrey, the Inspector said. A word.

Sure, Perkes said, his palms resting on the bar.

Perhaps at one of those tables?

Just wiped them down, Perkes said.

Tremendous.

Care for anything to drink?

Tonic water.

Coming up.

The Inspector reached for Audrey's drink, a rose-colored liquid with an orange rind floating on the surface. He raised her glass, breathed in.

Strong, he said.

I keep odd hours.

The work day is over then?

Ain't begun.

They sat opposite each other at a table built for four, the Inspector leaning over his drink, Audrey tilting back in her chair. Her auburn hair was cropped short, perhaps to better fit a wig; her skin was pale, her face marked with freckles. She appeared bruised, but had no bruises.

You look tired, he said.

The heat, she said.

Indeed. He produced a handkerchief from his pocket, wiped his forehead dry.

Would you like to see the body? he said.

What body?

I can take you to see it, if you like.

I don't know what you're talking about.

She wore a blond wig, young, maybe half your age.

Who?

I doubt she suffered. Whoever killed her held the gun inches from her skull.

You got me confused with someone else.

But you know who beat her, don't you? You know who put those bruises up and down her legs.

She rubbed out her cigarette, picked up her glass, set it back down without drinking.

The Inspector lowered his voice, reached for her hand.

Apart from Jonson, have there been any new clients in the last few days? Your answer is important. I'm trying to help your friend.

She hesitated as though waiting for an emotion to pass, then glanced toward the bar.

No, she said, pulling away. Apart from him there ain't been nobody at all.

The Inspector felt a hand on his shoulder, looked up to see Perkes smiling down.

Can I be of any help? he asked.

You have been, the Inspector said. He stood, pointed to his drink.

A tab, he said. I'll visit again.

He walked back to the bar, picked up his bag, rapped his knuckles against the counter.

By the way, he said, have any of you seen a boy? Between 13 and 15. He'd be on his own.

They looked at him, then each other, then their drinks.

I wouldn't let a kid that age in here, Perkes said.

I'm talking specifically about last night.

I worked last night. Closed the bar.

Gentlemen, the Inspector said, does Mr. Perkes speak the truth?

Yes sir, the man closest to the Inspector said. Every word of it.

• • •

The theater had been built to accommodate a metropolis that never materialized; judging by its remains, it might have covered a city block in any of the nation's smaller capitals. The ash had died in the desert air, the wreckage was more or less contained. There were people rummaging through it now, some with implements, some with bare hands, each operating independent of the others.

Hello there, the Inspector called. The nearest of them turned, spiked his pitchfork in the ash. He was abnormally tall, his legs rising to the Inspector's torso, his shadow the length of any two men's shadows. Behind him a half-dozen people of disparate ages and body types were likewise busy shoveling and sifting through the theater's remains: an obese woman, her hair sheered off, a deep sheen across her scalp; a boy not ten years old and a girl several years his junior, their bodies covered in blackened burlap; a female dwarf with fingers as long and thick as the Inspector's; a middle-aged man who was missing a hand yet seemed to wield his shovel more adroitly than any of his two-fisted colleagues.

Care to join us? the tall one asked.

Asthma, the Inspector said, holding up his badge. Just need to ask a few questions.

The tall man stepped clear of the wreckage. The others followed.

The manager has put you all to work? the Inspector asked.

A wage is a wage, the fat woman said, the sweat turning her cotton smock a darker shade of blue. And we got burned out of our booking.

What is it you're looking for? the Inspector asked.

Anything that shimmers, the dwarf said.

I'm interested in a boy, the Inspector said. He worked with his father, a man named Jonson. They sang and danced.

Worked? the tall man asked.

The father's been murdered, the Inspector said. The boy's missing.

The bald woman put her arm around the dwarf, the tall man crossed himself, the man with one hand registered no expression, the boy and girl seemed not to understand. The girl was fine boned, delicate, likely beautiful beneath the grime that obscured her features. The boy was unremarkable—round faced, gangly, like any boy one might find playing in a field or an alley. The Inspector hunched toward them, smiled.

We need you to keep digging, he said. It's important work.

But we haven't found anything, the boy said.

Then whatever is there to find remains hidden, the Inspector said.

That sounds like a riddle, the girl said.

Riddles aren't real talk, the boy said.

Go, the fat woman said, slapping her palms together. The Inspector waited, then continued.

Did you know them well? he asked.

Well enough, the tall man said.

Hardly at all, the fat woman said.

More by reputation, the dwarf said.

The man with one hand said nothing. He seemed anxious to get back at it, his heels raised off the ground, the fingers of his surviving hand gripping and releasing the shovel.

Reputation? the Inspector asked.

The boy was big-time talent, the dwarf said. The father was just sober enough to know what he had, but not sober enough to make it work.

And that you know by reputation, or observation?

Well, we all observed them yesterday, the fat woman said.

Yes, I heard. Did that sort of thing happen often?

Only all the time, the dwarf said.

Were they close, father and son? Did you know them well enough to know that?

Hardly, said the tall man.

You hardly knew them well enough? Or they were hardly close?

I never saw them speak two words to each other, except onstage, the fat woman said.

What about you, sir? the Inspector asked the man with one hand.

His father beat him, the man said.

You're sure? the Inspector asked.

You ever know a drunk who didn't beat his kid?

A few, the Inspector said. Let me ask this: was he close with anyone else? Is there someone he might turn to if his father were hurt? Family? Friends? Colleagues?

Didn't have a person in the world, the dwarf said.

Had a place, though, said one-hand.

What do you mean?

Chicago. The kid loved Chicago. He half-smiled, wide enough for the Inspector to glimpse blue streaks bleeding upwards into his bottom teeth. He couldn't wait for his old man to get tight so he could go out on his own. Walked that city front and back. Anywhere you went, there he was.

All right then, the Inspector said, pocketing his notebook. If any of you see him, you'll let me know.

Is the boy in trouble? the amputee asked.

I can't be sure until I find him, the Inspector said. But since you seem to have known them best, I'd like a private word.

I doubt there's much I can tell you.

Anything would be of value, Mr...

Swain.

The Inspector stepped to the side, cupped his hands to his mouth: Happy digging, he called to the children. He took Swain by the crook of his whole arm, led him across the street, stopped beneath the wooden awning of an empty storefront. They stood for a moment, Swain looking at nothing at all, the Inspector looking at Swain. He wasn't big, but he had a laborer's frame— squat, thick, a slight bulge at the waist. The half-circles beneath his eyes were inflamed with age and sleeplessness. He shuffled his feet, shifted his gaze, seemed to suffer from the kind of ner- vousness that comes with bad living.

Mr. Swain. Tell me, did the father have any enemies?

I don't know if he had enemies, but I couldn't say he had friends.

Why is that?

He was a drunk.

Yes, I know. What else?

Well, he was nasty. His mind was half gone, but he had a gift.

For?

For finding where a person was raw.

And exploiting it?

Every chance he could. But not because he wanted anything. Just for his own pleasure.

True, the Inspector thought, to a point.

It sounds like you speak from experience?

We all experienced him.

So the two of you had no particular quarrel?

No.

But you believe he was killed in anger?

Maybe. I hadn't thought about it.

But then why kill the woman too? Why not wait until Jonson was alone?

He wouldn't ever be alone. The only time he sent the boy out was when he had a whore coming.

The Inspector stopped himself from asking how Swain knew the woman was a prostitute, why he'd registered no surprise on learning there was a woman of any kind.

About the boy? the Inspector asked. He seems to have run off. Is there a chance his father made him angry?

No, Swain said. No chance at all.

Explain.

He didn't care enough about his father to kill him.

I'm sure it appeared that way.

. . .

A barker in a worn cadet jacket stood out front bellowing a list of attractions. The Inspector held up his badge, said he needed to speak with one of the performers. The man directed him to a second entrance off the alleyway; from there, a stagehand led him into a cellar crowded with cubicles fashioned from cloth scrims.

This one's his, the stagehand said, sliding back a curtain. Jonson's son sat on a wooden barrel, dressed in his underclothes, outfitting an old pair of English Brogues with a new set of laces. He didn't look up.

I have a message from your father, the Inspector said. He won't be able to make it tonight.

The boy nodded, said nothing.

You don't seem surprised.

The stagehand snickered.

I'll be all right, the boy said.

Yes, your father told me. Don't you want to know where he is?

I know already.

What else do you know?

About what?

About how your father earns his living?

He earns it onstage. Same as me.

I understand, the Inspector said. Would you do me a quick favor? Would you smile?

Smile?

I'd like to see your teeth.

The boy set down his shoes, pinched his lips and held them back while the Inspector leaned forward.

All clear, he said. It seems odd, though, that you didn't ask why I would want to see your teeth. Perhaps you knew that already, too?

He exited the cellar, walked a block in the direction of his apartment, then turned back.

The acts went by quickly. A hobo told jokes while sawing his wife in half, a small child ate knives while levitating a foot off the stage, a contortionist disappeared inside a wooden bucket. The Inspector wanted to applaud, but he couldn't help seeing the wire that held the boy in the air, couldn't help noticing that when the strong man dropped his weights they made no sound. Instead of feeling transported, the Inspector found his attention focusing inward. He was not, he thought, that different than the people onstage. Like them, he appeared skilled but was not expert in anything. An expert would be able to predict the outcome of his actions. The fact that the Inspector solved one case meant nothing when the next one arrived.

It was Jonson's son who brought his attention back to the stage. The boy could sing, dance. From atop his barrel, he executed acrobatic maneuvers at a speed the Inspector would not have thought possible. Jonson, with his curved spine and bloated abdomen, had spoken the truth at least one time: his son was more than half their act.

• • •

The air was beginning to cool; the moon, perfectly halved, hung as though designed to light this street. The Inspector heard a single pair of footsteps echoing toward him from behind. He stopped, turned.

Sir, a man said, the toes of his shoes now abutting the Inspector's, they ain't told the truth.

Who's that?

Them at the bar.

The man squinted, kicked the ground, scratched at the acne

rising from his beard.

All right, the Inspector said. OK. Let's talk.

He took the man's elbow, tugged him toward the nearest alley.

That boy was there.

I figured as much.

Last night.

OK.

He sang.

Quiet now, the Inspector said. We're almost there.

The man planted his feet, shook himself free.

I'm trying...

Walk, the Inspector said, grabbing the man's collar. Hurry now.

But already he heard a woman's heels striking the wooden platform behind them.

Arney, she called.

The Inspector turned, held up his hand, exhorting her to come no further.

Arney, Audrey said, I've been looking for you.

Her spirits seemed livened by alcohol. She'd applied her make-up, pulled a blond wig tight over her scalp.

Arney, stay with me, the Inspector said.

Audrey stepped between them, knotted her arms around Arney's waist.

I got some time before I start work, she said.

Yeah, Arney said: confused, ashamed. She reached up, kissed his cheek.

Audrey, the Inspector said, this isn't the way.

Do you have any time, Arney? she said.

The Inspector stared past her.

I can protect you, he said. The arm of the law reaches far.

Yeah, Audrey said. But Arney and I ain't far. Are we, Arney?

Arney allowed her to take his hand, allowed himself to be led away.

• • •

That evening, he opened the door to his room to find Mavis standing there with a plate of smoked turkey and mashed potatoes in one hand, a brim-filled glass of milk in the other. He stepped aside, waved her in.

I ought to have brought a tray, she said.

Nonsense, the Inspector said.

She set the glass and plate atop the dresser.

Do you have a moment? he asked.

I suppose I do, she said.

Good, I need your help.

He glanced into the hall, shut the door. Mavis smiled: a co-conspirator.

You've lived in this town a long time? he said.

Lord save me, yes, she said. Ed helped lay those rail tracks. He made it this far, then wouldn't go farther. Wouldn't go back, either. Like something spooked him.

There are things I need to know.

Such as?

Who, besides you and your husband, owns the property in this town?

Originally, she told him, the railroad owned it all. The railroad created the town, but they were quick to see their mistake. They sold the hotel to Ed, the rest to a real estate company out of New York.

And your Sheriff? the Inspector asked. Your husband said that he passed. How?

A vagrant slit his throat, she said. Someone he brought in

for the night, most likely out of kindness. Sam was an old man. Now there's just me and Ed.

And there's been no one to take his place?

Who would want the job? Mavis said. Before last night, the only murder we had was our Sheriff's.

• • •

According to the man who worked the kiosk, the boy had attempted and failed to board the previous night's train. The Inspector thanked him, stepped outside. For a while he was the only one waiting. A single electrolier lit the platform. On the opposite side of the tracks he could make out creosote brush, a brace of ocotillo cactuses. The air was cool, the sky crowded with stars.

A man in a borsalino hat mounted the platform, stood at the far end smoking a clove cigarette through an opera-length holder. Soon afterward, the performers arrived, the adults carting their luggage on dollies, the children trailing behind. Swain was not among them.

He felt the train's vibration before he heard its whistle. Moving to the edge of the track, he saw the headlight approaching but could not distinguish the cars from the black landscape. He stepped back as it pulled in. The full train was barely longer than the platform, a commuter rail making provincial stops between larger stations. He watched the performers haul their belongings onboard, watched the shopkeeper sprint from the kiosk and exchange sacks with a man in a belltop hat.

The Inspector walked to the lead car, showed the conductor his badge.

Mind if I take a quick pass through? he asked.

Anything I should worry about?

I just want to make sure someone didn't get by me.

The only light came from the lamp outside. Apart from the show people, most of the passengers were asleep, lapped in coats or blankets with hats pulled over their eyes. They were all either shorter, taller, thicker, or fatter than the boy.

He nodded to the conductor, then lingered for a moment, searching up and down the tracks as the train pulled away. When he turned around, the man in the borsalino hat was still there, smoking. He took a last drag, tossed the stub onto the tracks, returned the holder to his blazer pocket and started toward the street. The Inspector followed, watched him climb into a two-tone Sports Phaeton and drive off.

II

Next morning, he found Swain back amongst the rubble, sifting and digging, alternating between rake and shovel. The Inspector stood on the periphery, called hello. Swain's skin shone yellow-sulphur against the soot.

I thought you'd be gone, the Inspector said.

Why would I be?

Your colleagues have left.

They aren't my colleagues anymore, he said.

You resigned?

It was a long time coming.

In that case, we should celebrate. May I buy you a drink?

At this hour?

The day is hot already. A moment out of the sun would do you good.

Swain hesitated, searching for an excuse. Finding none, he set aside his rake, waded through the wreckage.

Splendid, the Inspector said.

They walked to the bar in silence, the glass storefronts candent in the morning sun, the surrounding foothills boasting their fullest range of blues and greens. Perkes greeted them from behind the zinc, gestured to the table the Inspector had occupied with Audrey.

Tonic water? he asked.

Coffee. Black. And a mimosa for my friend.

Let me guess—on your tab?

Please.

You're not drinking? Swain said.

Perkes, the Inspector called, a pinch of scotch in my coffee.

They discussed the local climate while Perkes prepared their order, Swain eyeing the Inspector, trying to discern a motive, the Inspector smiling, attempting to appear as though he had none.

I'm sorry for the loss of your venue, the Inspector said. Given the size, it must have been quite an establishment.

I never saw it even half full.

Perhaps they will build one of a more appropriate stature.

Maybe, Swain said. It won't matter to me either way.

Right, the Inspector said.

Their drinks arrived. The Inspector ran a finger around the lip of his cup, watched Swain tilt his head and swallow. Swain was not, the Inspector thought, so far gone as Jonson: beneath the feigned resignation, there was something he continued to want for himself.

If I may ask, the Inspector said, what was the issue with your colleagues? Why was your departure long in coming?

I'd had enough, Swain said.

Of?

Swain sniggered.

Of dickering over my spot on the bill, he said. Of split weeks and sleeper jumps. After a while, a man stops hoping.

I understand.

I doubt it, Swain said.

The gruffness of his tone gave the Inspector pause, made him wonder if he did in fact understand.

My own abilities have been questioned, he said. I've seen

people advance at my expense. Before long, you begin to internalize the doubt. You're right to make a break. There is such a thing as a corrosive environment.

Swain scratched his scalp with his hook, lifted his glass, set it back down without drinking.

You won't believe me, he said. But I played the Majestic once.

In Chicago?

I had a wire act. I wasn't top billing, but I wasn't shut, either.

What happened?

I took a spill. There was a full house to see it.

Were you injured?

A broken leg. A lump on my skull.

And when you healed?

I never set foot on a wire again.

I see, the Inspector said.

Swain looked him over, furrowing his brow as though on the verge of forming an opinion.

See what?

There's someplace you want to get back to, the Inspector said. I know the feeling. I started in the big city. I'm not in the big city anymore.

Swain nodded.

Which city? he asked.

The biggest city, the Inspector said. New York.

So why are you here with me?

I've spent a lot of nights considering it, and I'm not sure I've come to the same conclusion twice. There were people I didn't get on with, though I didn't realize it at the time. At the time, I considered myself dedicated, unyielding. My colleagues saw me as arrogant and overbearing. Not that they ever told me.

They let you go?

They set me up to fail. They gave me a high-priority case, a case that should have gone to a more senior investigator. It was a random crime. Unsolvable. When I failed to solve it, they assigned me to foot duty on a bridge in the dead of winter. The message was clear: the length of that bridge was all the police work I'd ever know.

So you left?

I started over in what you might call the hinterlands. I've made progress, but most days I still feel like an exile. I had something very few people have: a clear vision, a path I was supposed to follow. My life since has felt like a constant and sometimes exhausting improvisation.

Swain raised his hook:

I'd know about that, he said.

The Inspector felt a door beginning to open. Interrogating Jonson had been work: any cracks the Inspector had managed to expose in his veneer only revealed a new facade. Like Jonson, Swain lied when the questions mattered, but unlike Jonson, he appeared incapable of withholding the more intimate details of his life.

But then, the Inspector thought, *the same could be said of me.* He looked across the table. Swain seemed to be thinking with him.

What does any of this have to do with your investigation? he asked.

Not a thing, the Inspector said. I'm taking an early break. I wanted company, and the locals aren't as friendly as I'd like.

They never are, Swain said.

There is one thing about the case that puzzles me, the Inspector said.

What's that?

Jonson's son. Why did he run off?

Are you sure he did?

He attempted to board last night's train, but the conductor wouldn't allow him unaccompanied.

Swain appeared startled, tried to hide his expression by finishing his drink.

I've imagined myself in the boy's place, the Inspector said. If my father were murdered, why would I alert no one? Why would I flee? You know him. Can you explain his mind set?

The boy is a prodigy, Swain said. Pure talent. I couldn't say how he thinks.

Weren't you a prodigy once?

A false prodigy. But if I had to guess, I'd say the boy had been looking to get away for a long while. His father was a hard man.

That sounds like motive.

No, Swain said. Just opportunity.

That's what I was thinking.

I'm glad, Swain said. Now I'd best get back to work. Thank you for the drink.

The Inspector lingered outside, watching Swain walk back toward the theater. He had a stinging sense of having done wrong—of having made a confidence that he would betray. In the long run, he told himself, he would correct the mistake he'd made with Jonson. He would see that Swain was sober before setting him back on the circuit.

• • •

The shopkeeper spread the new envelopes across the counter, examined the addresses one at a time.

Sorry to disappoint, he said. But there ain't a name here I don't recognize.

No apology needed.

You ain't been having much luck.

What do you mean?

That boy didn't show last night.

No, the Inspector said. He didn't show.

As he exited the store, he glimpsed a man on the opposite rooftop glassing the town's surroundings through an outsized pair of binoculars. The Inspector turned as though he hadn't noticed, walked a block toward the hotel and crossed the street. Looking back, he saw the two-tone Sports Phaeton parked a short distance from the store. He passed through an alleyway, reversed direction, climbed the fire escape to the roof where the man had been standing. When he reached the top, the man was gone, the door to the building's stairwell locked from the inside. He crouched next to a scattering of cigarette butts, peered over the ledge and watched the Phaeton speed into the desert.

He remained there for some time trying to work out who the man was and what he had been looking for. Were the suppliers still in town, or had he been left behind to clean up? Was he searching for the boy? Or was he keeping tabs on the Inspector? Whatever the case, so long as the suppliers maintained a local presence, there was an avenue to pursue. He crossed the roof, stood surveying the visible length of rail track. There were places a body could hide, or be hidden, in the scrub and brush.

He climbed back down the fire escape, continued forward, descended the small but steep slope that led to the tracks.

Jonson's boy, he called. If you can hear me, say so. You're tired. You're hungry. I'm here to help.

A few yards distant, a pair of gray, unblinking eyes stared out from a parting in the scrub. In the morning light, the tan muzzle and earth-colored fur camouflaged the animal's head so that the eyes seemed to be pointing out of the ground itself. But as the head came into focus he saw that the snout was too long and large to belong to a coyote or any breed of dog that lived wild in the desert. He kicked dirt at the corpse to be sure it was dead, walked on.

He climbed back up the slope, running his eyes over and under the brush. At the summit of the incline, he turned, called again to the boy.

. . .

The Inspector had anticipated a home in keeping with the manager's personality—gruff, solid, needing repair. Instead, he found a large, well-maintained cabin, the logs stained raw umber and chinked with a pristine-looking clay. Behind the cabin, a bajada sprawled in all directions. Dried-up yarrow dotted the yard.

The manager was out front, peening dents from a car panel with a small sledge hammer. He saw the Inspector, let the panel and hammer fall.

A beautiful spot, the Inspector called.

A bit out of your way, ain't it?

I was told you don't have a phone.

That's cause I don't like talking to people.

Then I'll make this quick. I thought I instructed you to abandon your search for the boy.

The manager rutted his brow, stepped closer.

I'm at home, ain't I?

So you don't know a man who drives a two-tone Sports Phaeton?

Not in this country. Why?

Because somebody is looking for the boy.

The manager snickered, seemed to be thinking it over.

They must not have faith in your abilities, he said.

Who's that?

The people who want him found.

The Inspector ran a palm over the back of his neck.

Care to explain? he asked.

They rented.the theater's basement for storage.

Do you know who they are?

No. A real-estate man made the arrangements.

What were they storing?

Don't know that either. The lids were nailed down, and I ain't the type to pry.

So why do you believe they're the ones looking for the boy?

Because you ain't the first to come visit me. A man was here yesterday asking about the fire. Said his employer had an interest in what had been burnt.

And you turned him onto Jonson's son?

I did.

With what proof?

I answered his questions, just like I'm answering yours.

There is a difference.

Maybe, the manager said. But if there is, it don't tilt in your favor.

Tell me how to get in touch with this man.

He didn't say.

You're lying. He'd want you to notify him if the boy surfaced.

He said he'd visit again. Didn't say when, though.

You'd best hope no one tells me otherwise.

. . .

Jonson had soiled himself during the night. He was pale, agitated. There were scabs where he'd scratched the hives.

How many times has your boy seen you like this?

Is this the shit that keeps you up at night?

Maybe. What did you spend the night thinking about? You know your son took the stage without you. I saw him. He's talented, but young. There are laws.

Go to hell.

The Inspector sat watching Jonson. The symptoms had set in even more quickly than he'd hoped. After a while, Jonson's eyes closed, his head nodded forward. The Inspector set a vial on the table and left the room.

An hour later, he found Jonson awake, alert, his skin clear of hives.

Proud of yourself? Jonson asked.

It appears you're feeling better. These past hours must have been difficult. I'm sure you won't be anxious to suffer a relapse.

You really going to arrest my son?

If I have to. There are homes for children whose parents are incarcerated.

I'll answer your goddamn questions.

For the remainder of the day, Jonson delivered facts without commentary, his voice churning at a single dull pitch. The supply, he said, was never replenished in the same place twice, the location never revealed more than a week in advance. Quantities and addresses were communicated in code. They could contact him, but with the exception of a twenty-four hour window surrounding his acquisition of the new supply, he had no way of contacting them.

• • •

Swain had cleared a wide patch of debris; his overalls were cloaked in soot.

We need to talk, the Inspector said, climbing into the rubble. Officially, this time. A boy's life is at stake.

What boy?

Jonson's son. He set this fire. They know.

Who does?

Don't pretend. You're digging to find what was burned.

What are you talking about?

The blue in your gums, the Inspector said. There isn't time. They are going to kill him.

Who?

Your suppliers.

Swain stepped backward, stumbled over a charred beam, remained sitting where he fell. For a while, he seemed to be concentrating, tallying figures in his head.

It wasn't the boy, he said.

It might as well have been, the Inspector said. Tell me how to find them?

Arrest me.

What for?

Arson, Swain said.

You think that will convince them?

I did it.

The Inspector hesitated, considering whether Swain might be telling the truth. But an addict would not torch the source of his addiction.

Why? he asked, extending a hand, pulling Swain to his feet.

I told you before. I'd had enough.

He slapped at his overalls with his good hand, evaded the Inspector's stare.

I mean why protect the boy?

I'm not protecting anybody.

Let me put it another way, the Inspector said. What is your relationship to the boy?

We worked the same bill.

Nothing more intimate?

It was a moment before Swain understood.

You're trying to get a rise out of me, he said.

Maybe. You wouldn't sacrifice yourself without a reason.

I'm saying it was me. Isn't that enough?

The truth would be better.

I don't believe the boy did it.

That doesn't explain your confession.

Swain dried his scalp with his sleeve, sat on the beam he'd tripped over earlier.

Were you listening? he asked. The boy has a future.

I see, the Inspector said. He lifted a handkerchief from his watchpocket, unfurled it atop the beam and sat beside Swain.

I have something of my own to confess, he said. I knew Jonson. I knew him in connection to his second occupation. He was providing me with information.

Swain stood, kicked at a scorched door knob. *A calculated movement*, the Inspector thought. *He's known all along.*

He told you about me, he said.

No, but you just told me a great deal. Are they still here?

Swain turned his head, said nothing.

You can help the boy, but it has to be now. Take me to them.

I can't.

If you care about the boy's future, the Inspector said, then tell me how to find them.

I wouldn't know.

Are you sure?

I set the fire, he said.

All right, the Inspector said. When I find the boy's body, you'll be the first to hear.

He stood, shook out his handkerchief, stuffed it back into his pocket.

How do I know it isn't you who's after the boy? Swain said.

Why would I be?

Jonson's dead. The son might know what his father knew.

The Inspector smiled.

You're thinking too hard, he said.

He turned, began wading back to his car.

I knew this wasn't about Jonson and a whore, Swain called.

• • •

At the Inspector's request, Mavis transferred him to the room just east of Swain's. The Inspector switched on the lamp, set his bags next to the bed, stepped back into the hall.

Jonson and his companion had been killed at roughly this time the night prior. The hotel was quiet, the clientele absent. The Inspector knocked lightly on Swain's door, waited, took a thin file from the tubing in his sock and used it as he would a key.

The air smelled like a full night of Swain's breath and sweat. The Inspector switched on the light, stood looking the room over. A first glance discovered two Swain's: one painstaking, the other slovenly. The painstaking Swain assembled a portable wardrobe, a rigging of metal pipe and rubber wheels which he lugged from city to town, town to city. He hung his stage outfits at evenly spaced intervals, arranged them by color from brightest to dullest. This same Swain carried with him a series of six custom-made valises, carnival scenes hand-painted front and back, expensive on a showman's salary. He lined them up by height, ran a chain through the handles and padlocked the ends together.

The slovenly Swain scattered his belongings—a near empty pouch of tobacco, a toothbrush with the bristles chewed away, a key chain that chained no keys, newspaper clippings stained with fish oil and mustard seed—across what bare floor the room offered. This Swain left his bed unmade, his underthings, clean and unclean, dangling from open dresser drawers. The clothes he'd slept in lay crumpled in the sheets. There was a blindfold spread across the pillow, wax ear plugs trapped in a crevice of the blanket.

The Inspector stepped farther into the room, stopping to study the juggler's costumes: a tri-color bodysuit, a frayed blazer with burlap stitched over the elbows, a ballplayer's uniform with the glove sewn to the sleeve. He felt inside the blazer's pockets, stuck his fingers in the glove, searched the fabric for hidden compartments, found nothing.

He knelt beside the valises, reached back into his sock for the file. He worked the lock's mechanism with the lightest possible touch, set aside the chain and lifted the first valise onto the bed.

The interior was customized to carry a juggler's balls, with four wooden slats built into either side. On one side the balls were striped, with a small metal hook affixed to each; the solid-color balls had no hook. He took one of these in his hands and shook it beside his ear. It was weightier than he'd anticipated, made not of rubber or wood, but of a substance akin to sandstone. He set the ball back in place, moved to the next valise.

Here he found six prosthetic forearms, each ending in a metal hook, each cordonned down and protected with linen. The forearms varied in color, likely to match the juggler's costumes; the hooks varied in size and shape, with some as big as a double fist and others only slightly larger than a walnut, some so curved they nearly closed off, others with just a subtle bend at the tip.

He uncordonned the demi-arms, lifted them one by one to the light. They were spotless, polished—no trace of sweat, no flakes of skin. He examined the interiors, found them crowded with small, cylindrical objects. Picking up a single prosthetic, he wedged his fingers inside, dislodged the tape and slid one of the objects down, letting it fall into the palm of his hand. It was a chemist's vial, three-quarters full of a silver-blue liquid, the glass warm to the touch, the rubber stoppers crimped with metal foil. Either Swain's supply had been replenished before the fire, or it had been replenished at Jonson's death. Whatever the case, the loss of his provisions would compel Swain to contact his patrons. The Inspector liberated the remaining vials, wrapped them in his handkerchief, pushed the handkerchief into his pocket. He recordonned the prosthetics, set the valise in place, slid the chain back through the handles.

• • •

An hour later, he lay on his back in his own room, fully clothed, tonguing bits of turkey and lumps of potato from between his teeth. He imagined the boy hidden beneath a bed, curled up in a crawlspace. At first there would be fear, a constant attentiveness made electric by exhaustion. But after a while his mind would settle, begin to drift. In his exhausted state his memory would flash on images he had not meant to conjure, moments for which he'd hated himself, a time when somebody had treated him with a kindness he'd rejected, a time when his father had stood over him and instead of anger he'd felt fear, a time when he'd been wronged and done nothing about it. With each image his insides would seize up as though he were forcing himself awake. But slowly his mind would turn from the past. He'd see himself in New York, sitting on a bench in a park surrounded by buildings, eating a lunch he'd bought from a street vendor, reading a review of his performance. Lying, standing, sitting or crouching wherever he might be, all life would begin to seem possible.

The Inspector sat up, inched to the edge of the bed, pulled a black binder from his briefcase and opened it across his lap. The binder contained transcripts of interviews, of phone calls, of every word spoken between Jonson and the Inspector. Reading through their conversations, it occurred to him that had Jonson remained obstinate, had he simply allowed himself to be arrested, he would be alive now, his blood clear of toxins, his son safe.

• • •

He slept without meaning to, awoke to the sound of a scuffle coming from Swain's room. He pushed himself up, pressed his ear to the wall.

There was a crashing, a scattering of objects, followed by cursing, a sustained muttering of consonants, as if the underside of Swain's tongue were grinding glass.

Silence, then a spate of pacing. Swain's weighted boots beating out a rectangle around the bed. An opening and closing of drawers, then the drawers themselves splintering against the floor.

The Inspector made out a full-bodied collapse on the bedsprings, a hollow moaning that went on until well after he'd closed his eyes.

III

By dawn, Swain was active again, or maybe active still, pacing with his boots on, rooting through his belongings, swearing as audibly—if less frequently—as he had the night before. The Inspector stood, pressed his ear to the wall, heard Swain's door draw shut.

He hurried into his pants and jacket, grabbed his day bag. From the top landing he could hear Swain rapping the knuckles of his good hand against the front desk, Mavis having secured the bell for the night. The Inspector started heel-to-toe down the stairs, stood on the last step, watching Mavis pad forward, a morning robe knotted loosely over her bed clothes.

What is it you want? she asked.

I have to make a call, Swain said. An emergency.

Best be, Mavis said.

She unlocked a drawer, withdrew the phone.

I'll give you your privacy, she said. But don't be long.

Swain waited until she was gone, then pulled a balled up paper from his pocket and flattened it against the counter. He cradled the receiver between his neck and shoulder, dialed, let the line ring.

Swain, he said.

I'm sorry. I know.

Something's happened.

I need to see him.

Yes.

Out front.

He set down the receiver, exited the hotel. There wasn't long to wait. A pickup drove in from the west, pulled out again before Swain had shut the passenger door.

A few miles from town, they turned off the highway and onto a plain dirt path. The Inspector braked, allowed them to gain some distance, then followed. He closed his right eye to the sun, continued a long way up a slow incline, steering around thick patches of mojave aster, desert lupine, pausing at the summit to survey his descent. The path led to a long and narrow cabin circumscribed by a wall of imported pine. Cars were interspersed with the scrub on this side of the wall, the Phaeton and pickup among them.

He coasted downhill, pulled off road. He could follow Swain inside, attempt an arrest. But if the supply were not there, he would only tip his hand. And then, judging by the number of cars, he would be outmanned. Still, if he failed to act, there was a chance that the people he'd been chasing would once again elude him.

He felt on the cusp of deciding when Swain exited the cabin with two men, both wearing straw hats and overalls, both taller and thinner than the man who had fetched him earlier. The Inspector watched them cross through the trees, saw Swain stumble, clutch at his side. As he climbed into the truck, the Inspector noticed that the prosthetic was gone, that the man directly behind Swain was holding a gun. At first he wondered why, and then he knew: Swain had again confessed to setting the fire.

Careless, he thought.

He had meant for Swain to reveal the suppliers, but he had not intended to put the man's life in danger. He shifted the Packard into reverse, maneuvered back onto the dirt path.

From the summit of the first hill, he watched them spin onto the main road, head away from the town, moving faster over flat terrain than he could on the uneven slope. Turning after them, he shifted to the highest gear, forced the gas pedal to the floor. The truck was again in sight when the Packard lurched forward, ceased responding to the wheel, went careering along the edge of a gulley. The Inspector pumped the brake, brought the car to a halt on the road's slim shoulder.

IV

Swain sits stiff-backed between the men who'd beaten him, his calves straddling the gear box, his ribs throbbing. His captors are city folk costumed in overalls and brogans. It's the outfits, Swain thinks, that make them appear uneasy. He glances up at the rearview mirror, sees the Packard is gone.

The driver stops at the summit of a hill. Larger hills extend into the distance; a sparse forest of pinyon and juniper descends the slope they have just climbed. There's a woodshed in a clearing a few yards off. The driver steps from the truck but does not cut the motor. His partner backs out of the cab, waves for Swain to follow. The air is cold at this elevation. Blue sky makes it colder still.

The driver stops before they reach the shed, holds up a hand. On the ground, he says.

What?

Now.

Swain hesitates. A heel buckles his knee, a hand grabs his collar, forces him down. He blinks dust from his eyes. There's a sting in the back of his neck, a sharp pain as the tip of the needle pulls free. He feels his pulse slow to nothing.

They drag him into the shed, prop him against a wall. A lock clicks shut.

By the time he calls out, they are gone.

. . .

His breathing remains labored though his heartbeat has steadied. The shed is no larger than an outhouse. With his back flat against one wall, he cannot extend his legs. Slant rays of light pass through gaps in the planks. Gazing up, he finds spider webs clogged with desiccated husks.

He stands, peers between the beams. A vista emerges through a cluster of knurled trees—the opposite side of a mountain valley, an arid landscape showing its dullest colors in the afternoon sun. He takes a half-step back, focuses on the structure itself. The wood is dry and withered, but the planks are sturdy. There is no distance from which to launch a kick, no room to dig his way free. The hinges sit on the exterior of the door. Had they not taken his prosthetic, he might have wedged the hook between two boards, used one for leverage and prized the other loose. He might have scraped at a plank until it was thin enough to cave with his hand.

He sits again, the back and sides of his shirt soaked despite the cold. He is schooled enough to know that the periods of lucidity will become briefer and less frequent as the substance moves through his blood stream.

. . .

The Inspector watches the truck recede, navigate a sharp bend, disappear. Cursing, he steps onto the gravel shoulder, walks the periphery of the car. Rubber sloughs from the rim of the back right tire. He kneels, finds a thick shard of glass embedded in the sidewall.

Stupid, he thinks, tossing his jacket atop the hood.

Idiotic, he says aloud, lifting the spare from the sideboard.

He crouches, lays his weight into the jack crank. His palms slip from the handle and he stumbles forward, tearing his trousers at the knee.

All wrong, he tells himself.

• • •

He slides a hand over his body, finds his shirt unbuttoned, his pants pockets turned out. Rising up on his elbows, he can distinguish degrees of darkness, silhouettes suggesting a distant window or lamp. He stands, scans the space in every direction, walks toward what he takes to be a crack in the masonry, though when he reaches it he discovers not a crack, but rather a thin strip of window where the gauze drape falls short. The window is small, the type one might find embedded in a door. He runs his palms over the surrounding wall, feels no knob, no hinges, no other pause in the stone and mortar. He pulls the curtain back. Outside, it is night. The light comes from a fire, a building ablaze in a large and otherwise abandoned lot.

He turns from the window. Flickering light plays over mannequin torsos, stacks of ill-sorted fabric, a littered drafting table. He finds a light switch, flicks it on. There is a moment before the room comes fully lit. He surveys the ceiling, discovers no bulb. He surveys the walls, discovers no door. *Since I am here*, he reasons, *there must be an entrance, an exit.*

The room ends in a burlap curtain extending from wall to wall, ceiling to floor. He starts back, stumbles over a toppled mannequin, turns sideways to pass between a heap of shoddy and rolls of cloth piled chest high. He stops at the drafting table, crouches, studies a series of drawings sketched on tracing paper—gems of all kinds and cuts, shaded with colored pencil, arranged in no discernible pattern, intended for no discernible purpose beyond the practice of sketching them.

He passes through a part in the burlap. The light from the first room does not carry to this second room. Instead, the large open space is illuminated by a single candle set in a small iron stove. He scans the walls, looking for a door or false panel. He searches the floor, the ceiling. Nothing. His eyes land on the only object in the room apart from the stove: a cot, centered against the far wall. From across the room he can make out a flounced bed sheet, a form beneath.

Hello, he calls.

The form does not answer. He steps closer, distinguishes a face but not its features. He claps his hands together. The sheet does not move.

He crosses to the stove, removes the candle—a fat chunk of wax with the wick burnt halfway down. He places it on his palm, allows the dripping wax to congeal on his skin.

He sits on the edge of the cot. The sheet is pulled to the neck. There is no pillow. He balances the candle beside the head. The features are masculine, but the face is made up like a woman's—false eyelashes, cheeks caked with rouge, lips painted pink, scalp covered by a blond wig. Beneath the mask is a person Swain recognizes, though from where he cannot say. He tugs the sheet up, rubs the edge against the dead man's skin. The make-up smears. Swain takes up the box of wine, tilts it back, sniffs at the mouth. White, long since fermented. He spills a little onto a clean patch of sheet. Soon, the cheeks are bare, the lips pallid. He pulls on one set of eye lashes. The lids rise above the orbs, fall back with a slapping sound when the glue gives. A dark pupil stares up at him. Swain leans back, studying this new face, trying to imagine it animate, a voice speaking through the lips.

There is nothing from the chin up to say how the man died. Swain grips the edge of the sheet between his thumbs and index fingers, hesitates, peels it back. The torso is bare, cast in shadow. He lifts the candle, holds it on the flat of his palm so that it hovers above the man's chest. A surgical scar passes diagonally between the nipples; the breasts are spotted with vermiculate moles. Below the sternum, an outbreak of pimples that Swain would not have thought possible in an old man. He lifts the candle higher, watches the flame play across a livid imprint at the base of the neck, a deep and continuous bruise.

He sinks back to the floor, sets the candle on the concrete beside him. The pace of his breathing doubles, as though he's breathing for himself and the corpse. The longer he thinks, the more he remembers. The more he remembers, the more frequently he returns to the notion that he murdered the tailor.

His calf muscles spasm. His mouth has gone dry. He reaches for the box of wine, swallows the dregs. Acid stings the back of his throat, clears the film from his tongue.

He stands, leans one knee against the frame of the cot, swings his other leg over so that he is straddling the tailor's abdomen. Hunched forward, he fits his thumbs to the blood-colored prints beneath the windpipe, wraps his splayed fingers around the gelid neck.

• • •

Asphalt turns to dirt as the road progresses deeper into the foothills. A few miles in, he comes to the first gate. He slows, pulls off. There is nothing to say how recently the gate has been opened. The Inspector follows the side road with his eyes. A half-mile distant, maybe less, it begins its ascent, disappearing into stub-forest, then reappearing higher up. He searches for dust clouds, for a glimpse of blue between the trees.

There is nothing to do, he thinks, but guess. At the very least, he will be able to survey the countryside from the summit.

He leaves the gate open behind him, pushes the Packard as fast as it will go. The slope is steep. He steers around small boulders, feels the tires spin over a patch of pebbles before gaining traction. The road seems to rise toward a single destination with no turn offs or side paths.

He reaches the vertex, stops, searches out his binoculars

from the back seat. Climbing onto the hood of his car, he turns a slow 360 degrees, glassing the landscape above and below. He spots a blue pickup on the highway, speeding toward town. He loses it in the trees, finds it again, manages to fix the cab in the lenses. Two figures, two straw hats. The bed is empty.

He grasps for the revolver in his pocket, but the truck is well out of range.

• • •

There's a moment before he understands that the vertical slants of light mark gaps between the shed's laths, before his palm on the dirt means he is entombed on a mountainside.

Hives burn his scalp. He tells himself it is OK. All symptoms will fade with the poison in his system. There are factors working to his advantage. His tolerance, for one. The only course of action is to wait. Were he to break free now, he would lose his way, fall prey to wolves, twist an ankle, end up writhing in a gulley, delirious. He will not oblige them. He will not panic.

• • •

A sustained period of calm in which he feels his body weightless, his mind clear. Looking back, he is able to see large swaths of his life set within a single frame. Early days walking a guywire in the alley behind his aunt's building. A summer on the boardwalk. A succession of circuits taking him from one coast to the other. Wherever his mind lands, he discovers a hope and contentment he did not experience at the time. He sees his life not as he always thought of it—as progression and regression, movement toward and away from a target—but as modulating textures composed of noise, scenery, weather.

The question, he reasons, is not if he can forgive himself for killing Jonson, but if he can forgive himself for not killing

Connor. Not the recent Connor, but the younger, more capable Connor. The quality that had kept him from killing Connor was the very quality Connor had used against him. But Swain had been young, a child. He cannot blame himself for failing to kill Connor unless he is also willing to blame the boy for failing to kill Jonson. If he were unwilling to forgive the boy, then he would not have killed the boy's father. By extension, he must absolve himself.

But he is not the boy. Anything he had managed to do, he had managed to do despite something fundamental in himself, something he couldn't name but had spent his life disguising. A compulsion to be great. A conviction that he wasn't up to the task.

He feels his head nod forward, jerks it prone.

Now is not the time, he tells himself.

• • •

He wakes to find his pants soiled, the roof of his mouth cracked. He cannot tell whether the landscape has gone silent or his hearing has failed, whether the light has faded or he is nearly blind. For a moment he is back in the tailor's room, lying on the tailor's cot. There is a woman with him, wringing out warm towels above a vaporous basin, layering them across his forehead, his chest. He pushes her away.

V

The Inspector fetched a tire iron from the trunk, beat on the lock's shackle until the hasp tore from its hinges. Jerking the door open, he spun his head at the stench.

Swain sat with his torso hanging limp between his knees, his face in the dirt. Insects scrabbled up the back of his neck. The Inspector slapped them away with a handkerchief, raised Swain by the shoulders and set him against the wall. No breath, no pulse. Crouching, he gripped Swain's ankles, dragged him into the light from the Packard's beams.

The face was rimed with blood, but the Inspector could find no wound. He spit into his handkerchief, scrubbed until the source of the bleeding became clear: Swain had hemorrhaged from his eyes, nose, ears, mouth.

Why like this? the Inspector thought. *Nobody would have questioned gunfire here.*

He wiped sweat from his brow with the heel of his palm, stood with his arms akimbo, waiting for his breath to slow. The Packard's lights revealed a clutter of human and animal prints, his own among them. He scanned the visible ground, discovered no vials, no syringe.

He worked the corpse back into the shed, secured the door with a small boulder. At day break he would return with the undertaker.

. . .

He stopped at the turnoff to the cabin, exited the car, examined a flurry of tire tracks, the most recent curving toward town. Swain's murder had served a second purpose: it kept the Inspector occupied while they crated their belongings and left.

Wrong again, he thought.

Armed with the vials, he ought to have arrested Swain at once. As a result of his effort to learn more, the murderer had himself been murdered; Jonson's patrons had fled.

He sat against the hood of his car, staring out at the desert, squinting dim patches of creosote brush into focus, trying to think of any course he might follow. There was the real estate company Mavis and the manager had spoken of. There was Jonson's missive to the browser. The first was no doubt a front; the second provided the likely destination of his most valuable witness. As Swain had observed, the son might know what his father knew. And then there was the arson, a sentence with which to bargain.

He paced alongside the car, an idea forming and reforming in his mind until it seemed more like a physical sensation than a thought: he could not pursue the boy. Why? Because Swain had confessed to the boy's crime? Because he'd sacrificed himself for a vision of the boy's future? What future could there be for a motherless child who'd discovered his father lying murdered beneath a prostitute?

But none of that matters, the Inspector told himself, maneuvering back behind the wheel. *My job is to track what has been set in motion.*

He pulled onto the road, drove as fast as the dark would allow. The hollow energy that had sustained him throughout the day was beginning to fade.

But I do more than track, he thought. He'd left Jonson

alone with a vial, stripped Swain of his supply. Now his job called for him to arrest the boy, lock him in a windowless room, perform an autopsy on his life thus far. The boy would stare blankly, as he had that night in the dressing room—a skill he'd practiced daily in his life with his father. The Inspector would push harder, challenging the boy's notion that he had been powerless, arguing that he was at least complicit in his father's decline. Some part of you, he'd say, wished your father dead. You'd given up on him. Did it ever occur to you that you might have helped him?

And then, a chance for redemption: You can help others like him. Other boys like yourself. The Inspector could do this, had made himself do worse, not for the greater good, but because it was his job.

The town's scattered lights came into view. The Inspector steered back onto the shoulder, cut the engine, remained seated behind the wheel. He shut his eyes, saw Swain's corpse. He shut them tighter, saw Jonson's corpse.

He stepped from the car, waited for shapes to solidify in the dark, then made his way to the double-strand wire fence that separated highway from ranch. Leaning his forearms on a post, he searched out the few constellations he could identify. An animal the size of a small dog jolted through his peripheral vision. He pivoted, found the brush still. Without realizing it, he began to whistle—stray, anxious notes. He made himself stop. Standing still, the air seemed abruptly colder. He stuck his hands in his pockets, felt the handkerchief filled with Swain's vials. He removed a single vial, raised it above his head, watched the silver-blue liquid incandesce in the faint light.

Seen from a distance, he thought, someone might mistake it for an animal's eye.

He prized the stopper free, drained the contents into the scrub, reached back into his pocket. He came to the last vial, held it balanced on his palm.

He tried again to think of anything he might salvage.

Epilogue

He'd been with the family for half a year before they played Chicago. A taxi took them from the station to the hotel, the father and his youngest son sitting up front with the driver—the boy, mother, and older son in back. They passed through streets the boy thought he recognized, crooked blocks lined with stone row houses, stickball games breaking up to let the cab pass. But then the driver veered into a part of the city he'd never seen, a neighborhood marked by skyscrapers and elaborate vitrines, the sidewalks clogged with people.

Their hotel sat across the street from a long and narrow park with a skating rink that served as an outdoor marketplace in the off-season. From the window of the room he shared with his stage brothers he watched a man on a bicycle weave in and out amongst the shoppers. Somewhere behind him, the mother was helping the youngest unpack. The older son crossed the room, tapped him on the shoulder.

My father wants to see you, he said.

Now?

When do you think?

Julius, the mother said, mind your tone.

In the adjoining room, the father sat folding his show handkerchiefs into pocket-sized squares.

Hello, son, he said, pushing a stack aside. How are you feeling? Not tired out from the trip?

No sir.

Tell me, are you hungry?

I suppose.

How do you feel about pork chops?

The boy scuffed at the floor with his heels, shrugged.

Splendid, the father said.

• • •

It was early for dinner, late for lunch. Apart from the staff, the restaurant was quiet. They sat across from one another in a booth by the window. The waitress brought them a basket of bread and a saucer of olive oil. The father ordered a gimlet.

This should help calm my nerves, he said. Believe it or not, after all these years, I still get jittery before a show.

The boy nodded. Only when the main course arrived did he understand that the father had something he wanted to discuss. The boy watched him cant in his seat, drag the tines of his fork through a mass of grits.

My wife and I have been concerned, he started.

About my turn? the boy asked.

No, son, he said. You're brilliant on the boards. You must know that.

He waited for the boy to speak or to nod as though he understood what was coming, but he only worked a pad of butter into his potato.

You've been with us for almost a full season now, the father continued. We can't help but notice that nobody has written to you. Nobody has visited you. You haven't asked to visit anybody. Did your father have people?

No sir.

Is there anyone we can contact for you? Anyone you would like to see?

The boy stared down at his plate. The father took a long swallow, patted his lips with his napkin.

Here is what most concerns my wife and me, he said. Onstage, it's as if there's no house large enough to contain you. Some nights I think you're going to fly up into the struts. But offstage... well, it's a different story. I'm not asking you to tell any secrets, but I want you to know that we're very fond of you. If ever there's something you want to talk about, please know that our relationship is more than professional. Do you understand?

Yes sir.

The father leaned forward, pressed his palms together.

Is there anything you'd like to talk about now? he asked. Any questions you might have? About anything at all?

The boy made himself look back at the father. He had no questions, only a feeling that nothing was real, not in his new life or in the one that was gone. It was as if he could see the world around him, but could not see himself in that world. This separation had always been with him, an invisible but undeniable fact. A personal fact, since other people seemed to experience life more keenly. He wanted to tell the father, but as he tried to form the words he felt as though he were submerged underwater, and the only way he could breathe again was to avert his eyes.

No rush, the father said. No rush at all.

• • •

That evening, the family clears the stage as the boy steps center for his solo. He stub-toe walks forward, leaps into a handstand, palms gripping the lip of the boards, then pushes off, somersaulting backwards, landing flush atop a mailbox. For a moment, as the blood settles, he believes his father is shuffling on a barrel beside him. He windmills his arms, but the motion of his own limbs startles him, and he teeters backwards, nearly falls. The trumpeter hits a deliberate wrong note, long and strident. The boy recovers, stares up into the calcium ray. The eyes blinking back through that dense light appear detached, remote, and for an instant the boy feels as if he is up there with them, watching himself from the galleries. During the final beats of his solo, he breaks routine, ad-libbing a balance act, mixing bandy twists and barrel turns, bucking until his body blurs. When it's over he is soaked through and trembling, and the crowd's ovation does not draw him back onstage.

ACKNOWLEDGEMENTS

The author would like to thank the following people and organizations for their support, guidance and generosity: Laird Hunt, Selah Saterstrom, Eric Gould, the Evan Frankel Foundation, his teachers and classmates at the University of Denver, Patrick deWitt, Erik Anderson, Diane Kimmel, Sean Dingle, Brian Evenson, Gregory Howard, Linda Bensel-Meyers, Stephanie Krause, Michael Kimball, David Gruber, Wesley Gibson, Maureen Brady, Peter McGuigan, Stephanie Abou, Rachel Hecht, Matt Wise, Nina Shope, and (especially) Robert Lasner and Elizabeth Clementson.